# THE
# REBEL KING

# THE
# REBEL KING

BY

## MELISSA JAMES

First published in Great Britain 2009
Large Print edition 2009
Harlequin Mills & Boon Limited,
Eton House, 18-24 Paradise Road,
Richmond, Surrey TW9 1SR

© Lisa Chaplin 2009

ISBN: 978 0 263 20616 6

Set in Times Roman 16¼ on 17¾ pt.
16-0809-56342

Harlequin Mills & Boon policy is to use papers that are
natural, renewable and recyclable products and made
from wood grown in sustainable forests. The logging and
manufacturing process conform to the legal environmental
regulations of the country of origin.

Printed and bound in Great Britain
by CPI Antony Rowe, Chippenham, Wiltshire

This book is dedicated to Rachel Robinson,
for going above and beyond,
and who made Charlie the hero he became.
Thanks to Robbie and Barb also,
and to Emily Ruston
for excellent revision suggestions.

# PROLOGUE

*Sydney, Australia*

BY THE time the crew truck screeched up the footpath, the bottom storey of the house was engulfed in flame. Roof tiles at one end had already buckled and were smouldering. The wailing siren of the fire truck seemed obscenely loud over the terrified confusion of people racing around. The night sky was alight, the tinsel of the Christmas decorations in the windows had turned to blazing flame, warming the faces of the onlookers—and seeing the avid interest on so many faces didn't make things better.

*That's the job.* Charlie Costa faced it as he'd done for years. He'd store the jumbled mass of emotions for later.

'We have a five-to-ten-minute window. Winder, Costa, gear up and go in,' Leopard, the captain, yelled for Charlie and his partner, Toby. 'Do a sweep for any signs of life. The rest of you, douse the house and grounds, and watch those trees. We have to keep the monster from leapfrogging to the surrounding homes.'

'The monster' was the name 'firies' gave the enemy. Charlie remembered the cold shiver that had raced through him the first time he'd heard it. Now it was a battle cry against the hungry destroyer that was the fireman's daily enemy.

'Dissect your internal conundrums later, Rip,' a deep, growling voice came from beside him. 'For now, we fight the Great Destroyer.'

'I'll ask how I can do all those things you said later on, O Grizz, Lord of the Dictionary.' Charlie grinned at Toby Winder, his closest friend. The joking camaraderie they shared in life-and-death situations—such as calling Charlie 'Rip', a nickname due to his legendary temper, and Toby 'Grizz', due to his six-foot-five, muscular frame—helped to defuse the tension.

'Let's rock and roll.' Charlie threw on the mask and strapped on survival gear. Covered by the guys shooting a storm of water and fire-retardant chemicals, he and Toby charged in. They didn't use the axe to break down the door, but shut what was left of it behind them. The other guys would find and close any open windows, and board up those that had already exploded. The less oxygen in here, the better chances for any survivors of this inferno, and reports had come in that there was a young family still trapped inside.

'It's a kitchen fire,' Toby reported into the two-way radio as he bolted through the smoke-filled living room. 'It looks like the gas oven wasn't turned off. It shot straight up through the ceiling to the second floor before it took hold down here.' He wasn't spouting his favourite polysyllables now; he was too worried. 'I'll go upstairs, Rip can take downstairs.'

'No,' Charlie yelled, following Toby to the stairs. 'If anyone was downstairs they'd be outside already. We go up together, and find the kids first, parents after.'

What he didn't say was that pairs had a greater chance of survival. With the risk of the floor buckling under Toby's bigger frame, no way in hell was Charlie letting Toby go up alone. For some reason he'd never understand, his being there to balance the weight usually kept the floor from going a little longer.

They found the first survivor sprawled in the curve of the landing. A young woman, presumably the mother, her arms outstretched to the top storey. Toby did a quick ABC of her condition.

'Get the paramedics in. She's not breathing, pulse weak and thready. She's going down fast.'

Charlie doused the stairs and carpet leading to the door with flame retardant, and moved all furniture that could burn. Toby dragged in a clean breath, turned off the airflow to his mask and began artificial respiration. They couldn't chance any flow of oxygen or even tanked air on her until they were all safely out of here. She wouldn't thank them if they saved her but killed her kids in the inevitable explosion.

A sharp crack, followed by a tearing sound, came as the woman was stretchered out. 'The roof's going!'

As one, the two men bolted up the stairs. 'Send in two more guys to buy us some time!' Charlie yelled into the radio.

Leopard yelled, 'Get out, both of you, and that's an order. It's gonna go!'

Neither paid attention. Charlie took the far end of the hall without discussing it with his friend. Toby knew. He was the bigger and stronger of the two, but Charlie was leaner and faster, with a better chance of getting through any runners of flame.

Without glancing at Charlie, Toby ran into the first room to the left and Charlie immediately heard him shout a directive. 'Ladders to the top bedroom windows!'

Resigned to the inevitable, the captain gave the order. They all knew these two never left a building until the last survivors were found. The way they worked was almost uncanny, which was why the Fire Brigade had kept them together after training. Knowing each other so well could be a handicap in life-and-death situations, but with Toby and Charlie their honesty and camaraderie, their brotherly love, and the way they read each other's minds, made them the best team possible.

Crouching, Charlie ran along the sagging carpeted floor of the hall. It was ready to fall. He jumped from side to side against the walls where the floor remnants would be strongest because of the support beams. Keeping safe meant he'd make it into the room at the back of the house.

He opened the door, slipped in and shut the door behind him to cut off oxygen.

Through the haze the room took shape slowly, but moving would change the landscape, and he'd have to start focusing anew. Thirty seconds later and the picture came to his stinging eyes: a white room, pink bed-spread, a Barbie doll's house. He yelled, a weird, muffled sound through the oxygen mask, 'Is anyone in here?'

Even through the roar of the approaching monster, his trained ears heard a tiny cough.

He shut down and ripped off the mask. Talking through it scared kids, and the suit was scary enough. 'Hey, sweetie, my name's Charlie. I'm a fireman.' He choked on the smoke that filled his lungs and throat in seconds, and breathed in clean oxygen before turning off the mask. He couldn't risk feeding any starters in the room. 'Want to see your mummy?'

Another cough, weak and unformed, came from under the bed. Diving under the quilt, he saw a tiny ball of curled-up humanity. She was dark-haired and sweet-faced, about three. 'It's okay, sweetie, I've got you.' He croaked into the two-way, 'Ladder to the back room, far left! I've got a kid!'

'Forty-five seconds!' Leopard yelled.

Replacing his mask to breathe, he did a quick check on her. The child was alarmingly limp. He wrapped a rope around her fast, ready for the transfer when the guys got to the window, but she'd stop breathing any moment. He lifted her into his arms with excruciating slowness.

It was the cardinal rule: never take off your mask to give to a victim, because you can't save someone if you're dead or unconscious. Doing this would risk not only his life but the lives of his team who'd have to come in to save him, as well as the child if he passed out. But she was little more than a baby. He'd had his life—hers had barely begun.

Hoping there were no sparks in the room to feed on the oxygen, he ripped the mask off, turned the setting to 'air'—too much oxygen right now could do her more harm than good if she had smoke inhalation—and put it over her face. Then, holding his breath, he turned to get out of the door—but the paint was blistering down the edges, and peeling off the entire centre of it.

Smoke was curling off the door handle, and seeping through. An explosion came right beneath him. The house was going. The floor sagged under his left foot.

'I need a ladder to the extreme right of top floor! I've got an unconscious child. He isn't breathing!' Charlie heard Toby yell again, his voice harsh too. Obviously he didn't have his air mask on either. Time was running out fast.

The floor started buckling beneath Charlie's feet.

Slowly, inch by inch, he spread his feet further apart, feeling it give way each time he moved. His feet began to burn through his boots. 'We're gonna make it out, sweetie.' Hearing a voice, even his own, gave him comfort when everything was going down. 'Our guys are the best.' He coughed. *Crouch low for air, idiot!* But he couldn't shift down; it would cave the whole place in.

He was about to choke. He couldn't risk the floor going with the motion. He must breathe now, or risk both their lives when he fell. He watched the baby breathe in, took the mask, breathed in and shoved it back on her face before she inhaled again.

No talking now. His world consisted of watching her breaths: in, take the mask and breathe, back to her, and count the seconds. Glass smashed in the room next door. The fire was in the back walls, and the window had burst. The monster was about to hit.

A whoosh of clean air filled the room. The door burst into glowing sparks as the fire leaped in to meet the oxygen. A voice screamed, 'Give her to me!'

*Thank you, God!* Charlie leaped for the bed where the window was. 'Take her!'

The bed sagged sideways as the floor collapsed under his weight. He passed the child over as the heat at his back seared him. The hairs on his neck withered and his skin was melting—he could actually smell his flesh cooking.

'Jump, mate!'

He could barely move; the heat, pain and lack of air had left him in a stupor. One hand gripped the window sash; the other made it. *Good. I can do this. One knee up...*

The bed lurched back into the maw where the floor had been moments before. His body jerked back, but his desperate fingers held on. 'Help,' he whispered as his hands lost strength and smoke filled his lungs, his nose and throat, his eyes...

Hands came out of the cloudy darkness, lifting him through the window into a safety harness to lower him to the ground. 'We've got you.' It was Leopard. 'You saved her, Charlie. The little girl's going to make it, and so are you.'

Charlie coughed and coughed; the fresh air hurt, because the hairs lining his airways were gone or damaged. 'Toby?'

'He's okay, he saved the boy. We've done all we can. Let's go!'

He knew by what the captain hadn't said that someone was dead.

Oh, dear God...those poor kids had lost their mother.

As he was winched to safety, he felt the flashes and glare of media cameras turned on him. He heard the words 'hero' and 'saving the lives of a family', but he couldn't answer questions or accept praise for doing his duty. He fell to his knees, coughed until he choked, then threw up: the body's instinctive way of clearing foreign objects.

The paramedics had him on a stretcher within two minutes, and he was on his way to hospital. He slipped into unconsciousness, knowing the 'what ifs would haunt him until he died. Maybe he'd done all he could, but a woman had died today; two kids had lost their mummy before they'd been able to have memories of her—and, in his book, that meant that all he'd done hadn't been enough.

# CHAPTER ONE

*Sydney, three months later*

'I'M THE grand what of *where*?' Charlie grinned at the grave solicitor in the panelled oak office in the heart of Sydney. 'Yeah, right, pull the other one, Jack. Now, why are we really here?'

His sister's hand crept into his and held tight. 'I think he's serious, Charlie.'

At the fear smothered beneath the shock in Lia's voice, Charlie's protective instincts roared up. Lia was pale; he could feel the tremors running through her.

He couldn't blame her. If this was on the level, this news could destroy his sister. After all these years of progress, she could slide back to anorexic behaviour to cope with the stress of what this stranger was telling them.

No way would he risk that. 'Come on, Mr

Damianakis. Tell us why we're here. You're scaring my sister.'

The lawyer smiled at Lia in apology, but his words didn't give Charlie any relief. 'I'm aware this must be a massive shock for you both. It was a surprise to us, too. The consulate contacted us after the story of your rescue of the children in the house fire.' Now the apologetic look was aimed at Charlie. 'They'd sent photos of your grandparents to every consulate around the world. You really are the image of your grandfather. The photo of you getting the medal for bravery led to an investigation which showed your grandfather's entry papers into Australia weren't on the level. The Greek records showed that the real Kyriacou Charles Konstantinos, who shared your grandfather's birth date, died in Cyprus in the second year of the Second World War, eight months before your grandfather arrived in Sydney in 1941 using the same certificate.'

'That doesn't prove anything but that Papou was an illegal alien,' Charlie argued. It was something he'd always suspected. Papou had always worked for himself, and worked for cash whenever he could.

Charlie frowned, realizing for the first time that Papou had built and paid for the house and everything in it with cash—a man who'd claimed to be the son of a humble bricklayer, and who had only ever worked as a carpenter. Where had the money come from?

'No, in itself it proves nothing—but it was a start.' Mr Damianakis shifted again in his seat, reacting to Charlie and Lia's obvious discomfort with the situation. 'Your father's name is the Marandis family name—Athanasius, like your great-grandfather, the twelfth Grand Duke. Your grandfather's medical records showed some family anomalies, such as the crooked little finger on the right hand, and the AB-negative blood type, which is usual in the male Hellenican line, but rare among Cypriots, and is not at all in the Konstantinos family.'

Lia's grip tightened on Charlie's hand, and he could think of nothing to say to comfort her. Damn, he wished Toby was here!

'And your grandmother's Italian heritage clinched it. When we contacted her family in Milan, got pictures of her at a young age and saw her resemblance to you, Miss Costa, we knew we had the right people.'

Charlie rubbed the healing skin on his neck, where the heat of the fire had gone right through the flame-retardant suit to melt the flesh. The fallout from that fire had done more damage than even he had anticipated. The media had followed him for days, trying to make him a hero. They'd followed him and Toby as they'd visited the kids in hospital, and had awkwardly tried to console the grieving father who'd lost his wife. If he hadn't been instructed by the service to do it, for the sake of donations and good political mileage…

Damn the entire brigade! Those kids had lost their mother because he hadn't been able to save her. If it weren't for the press turning him into something he wasn't, he'd still be living in happy obscurity.

Whatever happened now, he had a feeling that much was at an end.

Charlie jerked to his feet, bringing Lia with him. 'This has to be a joke. You have thirty seconds to tell us why we're really here before we walk out the door.'

'I am one hundred percent on the level, sir.' Mr Damianakis handed Charlie a document and a photograph. 'Here's the late Grand Duke's birth certificate, and his photo taken when he came of age, sir.'

Charlie looked down, fighting a spurt of irritation. No one had ever called him 'sir' in his life, and never like he was a grand 'what' of where.

It was a young Papou in the photo, no doubt of it; Charlie saw the likeness. He'd always been the image of his grandfather. His Papou, who'd always hated war and had only fought over the backgammon table, was dressed in full military getup, covered in ribbons and medals, and the legend said:

*1939. The 18-year-old Marquis of Junoar at his graduation from the Hellenican Military Academy, with his parents the Grand Duke and Duchess of Malascos.*

The birth certificate gave no reprieve: *Kyriacou Charles Marandis, son of His Grace, Athanasius, The Grand Duke of Malascos, and Grand Duchess Helena Marandis, née Lady Helena Doughtry, daughter of the Earl of...*

The words blurred in front of him as his head began spinning. The birth date was right; the face was exact. And he couldn't deny the name— Kyriacou Charles. It was his name as well as his paternal grandfather's name, in the old tradition, just as Lia was Giulia Maria, named for their grandmother, their beloved Yiayia.

If all this rigmarole was true, their shy, retiring Yiayia had been a count's granddaughter, an untitled royal nanny for whom Papou had given up his position to run off and marry, if Mr Damianakis could be believed.

He was descended from dukes and earls? He was a lost heir?

'So when do the man in the iron mask and the three musketeers show up?' he asked, with a world of irony in his voice.

The lawyer gave him a wry smile in return. 'It must seem unbelievable: the runaway duke, the lost prince and princess—a massive fortune.'

Lia had read the words on the photo over Charlie's shoulder and stammered, 'It can't be Papou. You have the wrong people. Our last name is Costa. We're Greek.'

'Your grandfather took the surname and nationality he was given by the man who created his false identity, and changed Konstantinos to the simpler version—Costa,' Mr Damianakis said gravely. 'Probably to avoid media scrutiny and being followed around the world. But there is no doubt. He became the Grand Duke of Malascos at his father's death, and you became the Marquis of Junoar when your father died. Due to the tragedies in the nation in the past decade, you are no longer merely the Marquis of Junoar or Grand Duke of Malascos.'

*Merely?* Charlie heard his mind shout in disbelief.

'But by Hellenican law, as the last male in the direct line, you are Crown Prince, heir to the throne. And you—' he smiled at Lia '—are Her Highness Giulia Marandis, Princess Royal of Hellenia. Your great-grandfather left a massive private fortune to his lost descendants, totalling over five hundred million euros in land, gold and in bank accounts. I think he wanted his son to know he'd forgiven him.' He rushed around to Lia, who'd turned alarmingly pale. 'Please sit, my lady.'

Lia released Charlie's hand and fell into the chair, her breathing erratic. 'Don't call me that,' she said, her voice horrified.

The room swung around Charlie in slow ovals: around and up and down, like he was in a crazy ride he couldn't get off. But he was a fireman, damn it, and he didn't fall down under shock. He strode to the window, saw the limousine with diplomatic flags on it, and clenched his fists. The fairy story he wanted to laugh at was crystallising into horrifying reality. 'You said the king and my great-grandfather disinherited Papou when he married Yiayia. So what do they want with us?'

'When your grandfather was disinherited, he was ninth in line to the throne, but there were another twenty direct members of the Marandis family to inherit,' Mr Damianakis said, in the tone of respectful gravity that killed Charlie's urge to laugh this all off. 'The past thirty years has been a tragic time in Hellenia. An attempted coup killed several members of your family. Twelve years ago rebel forces created civil war on behalf of the heir of a man in direct rivalry to the throne, named Orakis, in an attempt to reclaim it. The war lasted a decade. Thousands died, towns and villages were destroyed.'

Good God, now he'd gone from romantic legend to an item on the news networks. 'So if this Orakis guy wants the throne so much, let him have it,' he snapped. 'Then nobody else has to die.'

'Charlie,' Lia said in gentle rebuke. 'This isn't Mr Damianakis' fault.'

'Sorry,' he muttered with distinctly unroyal grace. He waved. 'Go on.'

'Not quite two years ago, the Prince Royal and his son contracted meningococcal disease and died within a day of each other, leaving only the Princess Jazmine in line for the throne. The laws of Hellenia do not allow for female inheritance if there is a direct male Marandis to take the throne. The Grand Duke of Falcandis is a descendant, but through the female line. King Angelis began a search for his first cousin, the Grand Duke of Malascos, and his descendants.'

Had they fallen down the rabbit hole? Charlie kept waiting for someone to jump out of a cupboard, yelling 'Surprise!'. 'Just call me 'Charming',' he muttered.

Lia chuckled. 'Yeah, like that's ever going to happen.'

He grinned at her.

Mr Damianakis spoke again. 'If you require further proof, sir, there's a limousine waiting outside to take you to the private jet waiting at Kingsford-Smith airport. It will fly you both to the Hellenican Embassy in Canberra. A representative of the royal family is waiting to answer any questions you have, and give you the papers you need for an immediate flight to Hellenia. His Majesty the King of Hellenia, as well as Her Royal Highness Jazmine, and the Grand Duke of Falcandis, await your arrival.'

As the lawyer said something else, Charlie's mind wandered. He shook his head, trying to clear it, to wake up and find he'd been knocked on the head. Half the time he barely felt qualified to be a fireman, and now he was…was…

Maybe he'd taken a hit by a supporting beam at that Christmas fire, or suffered brain damage with the smoke inhalation, and kept relapsing into delusions?

'Charlie…'

He turned on his heel to see his sister's cheeks holding the dreaded greenish hue. 'Lia?' He ran to her and knelt at her chair, checking her pulse automatically. 'What did you say to her?'

Damianakis licked his lips, distinctly nervous. 'You didn't hear me?'

'Would I need to ask if I had?' He heard the lash of impatient anger in his tone, felt Lia's hand press his, and tightened his lips. How many times did he have to shoot the messenger because he couldn't keep his temper under check? 'This isn't your fault. Just tell me what upset Lia.'

Damianakis shifted in his seat. 'I said you need to prepare yourselves. The ambassador thought it best that I tell you here, in a quiet environment.' As if gathering his courage, he looked up at Charlie. 'His Majesty, King Angelis, has arranged royal marriages for you both, to take place as soon as possible.'

*Orakidis City, Hellenia*
*The next morning*

The beautiful old black Rolls pulled up outside the front of the sprawling, four-winged mansion that was the royal family's summer palace, where the king was keeping residence until the main palace was fully repaired from a fire attack a few years before.

There were too many repairs still yet to make to the nation's towns, cities and homes for the royal family to think of repairing a palace as a priority.

Jazmine's heart beat hard as she stood beside Max at the foot of the stairs, four feet behind the king, as adherence to royal protocol demanded. As Princess Royal and the Grand Duke of Falcandis, they held positions the world would envy; yet here they were again, the king's dolls to rearrange as he wished. Old friends, they'd been engaged to each other until a month ago; now they were both engaged to strangers.

Was this a case of a magnificent escape for them, or being tossed from the king's frying pan into his fire?

'Courage,' the Grand Duke murmured in her ear.

She stiffened. A princess to the core, she'd had correct deportment and proper distance drilled into her since birth. 'This is my duty. I don't need courage to face what I can't change.'

His deep, smooth voice was rich with amusement. 'You're right—resignation would be more useful in our case.' He waited, but she didn't answer. 'Talk to me, Jazmine. Surely, as the most recent object of your duty, I can intrude on your pride and share our changed circumstances with someone who understands?'

She felt a tinge of heat touch her cheeks. Her grandfather, the king, had dissolved their engagement when the news of Prince Kyriacou's existence had been confirmed. His press secretary had hinted that childhood friendship made the engagement awkward: a truth His Majesty used when he found it convenient.

Jazmine smiled up at the fair, handsome face, so like his English mother. She'd been so embarrassed by her grandfather's dictum, she hadn't been able to look at him until now. 'You're right, Max. Thank you.'

'Here come our respective futures,' he murmured, smiling at her with the sibling-like affection they'd shared since she was thirteen. 'Our third or fourth cousins, or something. Almost not related at all, apart from the name.'

*Thank goodness*, Jazmine almost said aloud. She'd found the thought of marrying any relative revolting, but, with Prince Kyriacou's grandfather marrying an Italian count's grandchild, and his father marrying a Greek woman— a *real* commoner!—the lines had blurred.

Jazmine's mother had been of the Spanish nobility—more line-blurring still. The more the better, in her opinion.

She started as the trumpets of Grandfather's private band blared the national anthem of Hellenia—*In Our Courage We Stand*—in acknowledgement of royalty's arrival. It was odd, considering that no one else was there but family and royal staff.

A young woman emerged first, wearing the tailored skirt and silk blouse Jazmine had chosen. This was Giulia, no doubt.

No doubt at all, from the moment she looked up. Though she resembled her Italian grandmother, Giulia was a complete Marandis. She had willowy curves, thick dark curls tumbling down her back, the heavy-lashed, slumberous eyes, the deliciously curved top lip. On the Marandis women, it looked like a hidden smile waiting to burst out, a wonderful secret they wouldn't tell. Tall and graceful and golden-skinned, Giulia was beautiful in the quiet, understated, Marandis way.

Then her brother emerged from the car, and Jazmine heard the death knell of her plans before she'd even been introduced to the prince.

Oh, he was handsome—dark, lean and oozed

hot sensuality. But he was no story-book prince come to win the princess's heart, and—her heart sank—she doubted he ever would be.

Thick curls cropped short, dark eyes and the regal nose. Yes, Kyriacou was as much a Marandis as his sister, but on him it didn't achieve elegance. In the charcoal Savile Row suit supplied for him on the jet, with the white shirt and sky-blue tie, he didn't look suave, he looked turbulent. Every inch of him was lean and muscled, big and fit—'buff', her friends from Oxford would have said. She might have said it herself, if she wasn't a princess.

And, if he weren't a Crown Prince, she'd call him hostile.

He looked as regal as a lion, ready to attack, as frighteningly compelling as a wind-tossed storm cloud about to unleash a torrent.

Yes, that was it exactly. God help her, she was engaged to a wild beast set to pounce. And the windstorm was about to break right over her head.

Well, she was used to flying in storms, and flying blind. Five years ago she'd been a minor royal, then after the civil war had ended, she'd become Princess Royal. She'd become the unwanted, 'couldn't-inherit' female heiress two years before. She'd been engaged to Max until a month ago; now she was engaged to this stranger.

If she'd had a choice, she'd still have taken this fate for the sake of her country and her people. She'd make this man want to marry her, unless she wanted to create an opportunity for Markus Orakis to seize the throne.

Hellenia had seen enough of coups, civil war and murder to last ten generations. She'd do whatever it took to end the bloodshed, to help this country heal from its scars—and she'd cope with this Marandis the same way she coped with her grandfather, the king.

*Keep your dignity. Don't let him walk all over you. When you give in, do so with grace. You are a princess, no man's doormat.*

If only it didn't sound like a fairy tale in her own mind. No matter how much she wanted to be her own woman, she, like Max—like the new Marandis brother and sister—was a servant to the crown, here to bend to the will of king and country. If Kyriacou and Giulia Marandis didn't understand that, they soon would.

The new Crown Prince and Princess Royal walked through the line of saluting king's guards, and beneath the meet-and-kiss flags showing the royal scarlet-and-gold over deep turquoise that was the symbol of Hellenia, and the Marandis banner: the soaring royal eagle over verdant hills and valleys. A massive bouquet of white roses was thrust in Giulia's arms: the flower of peace.

Grandfather stepped forward, every inch the regal ruler. He extended his hand towards the brother first—the expected way in this male-dominated society. 'Welcome to Hellenia, Kyriacou,' he said, using the traditional first-person version of the name Kyriacou, making it more personal, intimate. 'And to you, Giulia.' With an attention to detail he'd never lost, the king pronounced her name with beautiful precision: *Yoo-lya.* He smiled warmly. 'Welcome to our family, and to your new home.'

Neither responded for a few moments. Though she smiled, Giulia's face held a look of bewildered wonder at the change in her status. Kyriacou held his sister's arm in obvious protectiveness. He didn't move to take the king's hand, or bow in response to the traditional but sincere welcome.

'My name, *sire*,' he said clearly, 'is Charlie.'

# CHAPTER TWO

STUNNED silence reigned at the flagrant breach in royal protocol.

Breach? It was more like an abyss. Nobody spoke to King Angelis like that, or refused his hand. Hadn't Eleni taught them the correct mode of address while on the jet? Jazmine had sent her own personal assistant to Australia for that sole purpose.

Giulia stepped forward with a gentle smile, placing her hand in Grandfather's. 'Thank you, your Majesty.' She dipped into a deep curtsey. 'Forgive us. We're still confused by the changes in our lives, and tired from the long flight.' She lifted her lovely face, smiling. 'We're not used to this level of fuss attached to our arriving anywhere.'

Jazmine relaxed. At that moment, she knew she'd like Giulia. She was a peacemaker who knew how to keep her dignity and courage.

It was a good thing. Marandis women needed to be strong to survive.

Seeming mollified, Grandfather smiled again. 'Well, at least you listened to the procedures for royal protocol on the flight.' The look he slanted at Giulia's brother was frost itself. Pure snow.

'Pardon me for being underwhelmed by thirty-six hours spent in lawyers' offices, limousines, consulates and jets. We were forced to leave our home and life without warning, pushed into limos and jets without consent, told we had to obey the will of a king we knew nothing about. We've been bowed and scraped to wherever we go, "Your Highnessed" to death, had "this is a royal secret" slammed into us every thirty seconds. If I was given any choice in any part of the past thirty-six hours, I might have *chosen* to listen,' Kyriacou—Charlie— snapped. 'I'm not a puppet whose strings you can pull, and it would be good for you if you remembered that…Your Majesty.'

More silence, as everyone held their collective breath, waiting for the king's reply. If Jazmine didn't have self-discipline, she'd have closed her eyes. The new Crown Prince of Hellenia was a moron, unable to follow simple instructions or to know one always respected royalty.

Grandfather's eyes narrowed. 'You will learn differently, Kyriacou. My word is law in Hellenia.

I can force you to return to your obscure life without the benefit of your great-grandfather's fortune. Don't embarrass me publicly, boy, or you'll regret it.'

'With respect, Your Majesty, bring it on,' Charlie returned without a blink, or lowering his voice. 'I was enjoying my life until yesterday. Obscurity and the single life suit me right down to the ground. Maybe you should find a new heir, Your Majesty, because I'm nobody's idea of a duke, let alone a prince—and bringing me here is the furthest you'll manipulate me.'

It took all Jazmine's self-will not to gasp. Instead of being intimidated, the new heir met ice with fire—and a tiny part of her, the rebel she'd submerged years ago, wanted to cheer him on.

Maybe he wasn't as stupid as she'd feared. And maybe there were possibilities in this. If he could stand up against the old autocrat and hold his own, he could be perfect for her purpose. If she could bring him to see what he could accomplish for Hellenia…

Her brain began buzzing with plans.

A royal staffer stepped into the breach, performing his assigned duty with no sign of discomfort. Every inch the Oxford-trained gentleman. 'Your Royal Highnesses, may I intro-

duce you to Jazmine, the Princess Royal, and
Maximilian, the Grand Duke of Falcandis?'

Perfectly done. His name was not to be men-
tioned until the important personages were introduced. Diplomats and royal staffers knew how
to blend in.

'Your Highness.' Giulia dipped into another
curtsey. 'Your Grace.'

Max smiled but remained silent, waiting for the
first in precedence to speak.

Jazmine smiled with genuine pleasure at Giulia.
'Please don't curtsey to me. And call me Jazmine.'
She kissed Giulia's cheek with warm welcome.

Giulia smiled back. 'My father was an only
child, and my mother's relatives were all still in
Greece, so I've never had a cousin, Jazmine, but
I've always wanted one. My brother tends to be
a bit overprotective.' Those glorious eyes
twinkled at her brother, who merely grinned. 'My
friends call me Lia.'

It seemed their lives were more alike than
Jazmine had anticipated. She too had grown up
with her relatives far away; she too had lost her
mother at a young age, and had longed for a
friend, a confidante, who *belonged* in her life.
'Perhaps we should be thinking of each other as
sisters, Lia.'

'I'd like that.' Lia's face lit, as if Jazmine had offered her a fortune.

Without warning, her throat thickened. How long had it been since she'd had a simple offer of friendship from a person she could trust? But, much as she wanted to explore a friendship with Lia, her duty wasn't complete.

With some trepidation she turned to Charlie, allowing none of her concerns to show in her face or voice. 'If you don't mind, I'd rather not think of you as a cousin, Charlie.' She held out her hand to him. 'I don't think it would bode well for the future.'

To her surprise the new prince took the extended hand, and grinned as he shook it. He drawled in a mock-Southern accent, 'Smacks too much of hillbilly movies and all them there in-breeders?'

Caught out, she did laugh this time. 'Well, we're only third cousins.'

Suddenly Jazmine needed a long, cool glass of water. Her mouth and throat had dried, watching that dark, dangerous face soften with the sexy Marandis smile. His voice was rough with the Australian twang, deep and intensely masculine. Suddenly it made the cultured accents of the men she knew sound, well, namby-pamby. And she was having the strangest reaction to the feel of his hand in hers.

For the first time in years, her self-control vanished and she had not the slightest idea what to do or say.

'Don't worry,' he whispered softly as he pretended to kiss her cheek. 'This isn't your fault. I'll find a way out of this crazy situation.'

She blinked, stared, opened her mouth and closed it. Where had her famous self-composure disappeared to when she needed it?

Max's smile told Jazmine he'd seen her reaction to the new prince. Taking the focus from her, he moved forward to meet the new arrivals, shaking hands with the right degree of friendly welcome.

'We will take tea.' The king turned towards the stately sandstone house—the Marandis summer palace since the eighteenth century—before anyone else could speak.

The smile vanished from Charlie's face. He nodded, as if his permission had been sought, and turned to walk with Lia into the house.

Despite his being a firefighter, obviously taking orders wasn't something he enjoyed, though he seemed to know to choose his fights and bide his time.

Though that meant more work whipping him into shape, the complex nature of the new prince seemed to fit into her very personal agenda for the future of Hellenia. A modern hero with rebellious tendencies—as shown by his rescue of the children in Australia—and knowing when to keep silent, was exactly what her people needed.

She turned to follow her grandfather, taking Max's arm. Then she remembered, and turned to Charlie to walk inside first. He was Crown Prince now, and above her in station.

He took his sister's arm and stood, waiting. 'I was brought up to allow ladies—and princesses—to go first.'

The words told her more than she wanted to know. He had no intention of accepting the title, or becoming a part of the royal family. He wanted to return to Australia as soon as possible. He'd soon learn it wouldn't happen. Royal families didn't belong to themselves, or have the luxury of independence.

As Max took her arm, he whispered, 'I suspect life is about to get interesting. Our new prince is a firecracker. Good luck with that.'

She stifled a laugh. 'I suspect you're thanking the gods for your changes, now you've seen Lia.'

'She certainly is lovely,' he murmured, 'And smooths over the waves. Good manners and well brought-up. Just what every man wants in a wife.'

Jazmine caught the irony in his tone. If Max

resented being a slave to royal duty, he hadn't shown any sign of it in the past few months—but then, how could he until now?

'If the sister was well brought-up, what happened to the brother?' she whispered.

'By all accounts, his grandfather never bowed to the will of the crown,' Max replied, just as softly. But as they passed through the grand double doors to the ballroom-sized chamber known as the tea room, she saw Charlie stiffen.

Max ushered her into the room. 'Well, you can't fault his hearing. You might want to keep any future liaisons—'

'I'm not biting.' She smiled sweetly at him. A prince in waiting and a gentleman to the core, Max had always enjoyed putting the cat among the pigeons.

Max grinned. 'You can't blame me for trying. It doesn't appear as if my future bride has the Marandis fighting spirit your future king has in spades. I fear she'll make me a poor opponent.'

Jazmine shook her head. Having read the investigative reports into the brother and sister, she doubted Lia lacked anything, including spirit. Her story of anorexia survival proved that, but Max would have to find out in his own time and way.

Grandfather waved them all into chairs facing

him. By the way he drew himself up and refused to sit, he was about to hold court, as he called it.

She called it laying down the law.

'Tea,' he ordered a servant, who bowed and disappeared. The room emptied.

To Jazmine's surprise, Charlie took a seat beside her. He was glancing from her to Giulia—who sat on Jazmine's other side—but his expression didn't change. He still looked grim and protective.

'We will have no public displays in future of family discord, Kyriacou.'

Grandfather never descended to such terms as 'do you hear me?' As king, he could enforce his word with the full force of the law, even in the twenty-first century. He believed the Hellenican people liked it that way.

Jazmine had other ideas, but they'd remain her own until she was queen. *If* she became queen. She kept her gaze on the man who held her entire future in his hands.

Charlie was sprawled in his chair, watching her grandfather with polite interest, as if the king was an unusual exhibit at the zoo. 'It's been a long time since anyone defied you, I'd guess, Your Majesty.'

Grandfather put a hand on the back of the carved-oak chair. His brows lifted a touch. 'Certainly.'

Charlie said politely, but with finality, 'Well, here's the lowdown on *family discord*, sire. I'm not your family. I met you *five minutes* ago. I am an Australian citizen—'

The king's smile stopped him mid-sentence.

'Actually, Kyriacou, you are a Hellenican citizen,' Grandfather stated with well-bred relish. 'You are a descendant of the royal family. You have been Hellenican, subject to its laws and regulations, from the moment you stepped into the consulate in Canberra.'

The silence was absolute. Even the servants didn't breathe.

After a minute that seemed to take an hour, the king went on. 'My word is law in Hellenia. You will do as I tell you, and leave only when I allow it.' He smiled at Charlie in barely re-strained triumph.

Giulia's face was pale as she turned towards her brother. Max lifted his brows.

Jazmine felt herself gulping on air. Whatever Charlie said or did, unless it was capitulation or an abject apology, would only throw a landmine into Grandfather's proud, stubborn face—and, on five minutes' acquaintance, she felt sure 'capitu-lation' and 'apology' were words as foreign to the prince's nature as they were to the king's.

After an interminable minute, Charlie answered without the expected fire. 'Without prior knowledge of Hellenican law, we've been subjected to false imprisonment, which is subject to international law under the terms of the Geneva Convention.' He smiled back at Grandfather, whose lined, regal face whitened. 'You made a mistake in underestimating me, Your Majesty. I will not be forcibly detained here. Nor will I allow you to force my sister or me to accept the positions. We are not political prisoners. If you make us such, I'm sure the world media would love to know about it.'

War declared—and it was about to be accepted. Before she knew it, Jazmine was on her feet, looking down at Charlie. 'May I speak with you, please, Your Highness?'

Arrested by her intervention into the hostilities, Charlie turned and looked at her. A brow lifted as he searched her eyes. Jazmine's panic grew as he seemed to be looking past her projected calm. Seeing more than she wanted him to.

'Of course, Your Highness. I'm at your service.' Just as slow, seeming almost insolent, he rose from the chair, stood and held an arm out to her as he'd seen Max do.

He was a quick learner when he wanted to

be…but the challenge in his eyes told her the changes would come only in his time and way.

This man definitely had hidden depths—and, as he'd said to Grandfather, it was a mistake to underestimate him.

'Do the goons get in line every time you move?' he said in a conversational tone as they headed to a parlour, and four Secret Service people followed at a discreet distance.

'Actually, two of them are yours. They're here to protect you.' Resisting the urge to pull her arm from his—the Secret Service would report the disharmony to Grandfather—she checked his reaction.

*Bad* mistake. The brows were up over laughing, derisive eyes. 'Protect me? A little, five-foot-four Miss Perfect is going to take me down? I need help handling *you*?'

She nodded at their combined minders to step outside, then closed the parlour door behind them. 'I'm five-foot three,' she retorted, intensely aware of keeping her dignity. 'And, though we both know it isn't me you need protection from, I have a green belt in karate.' She could also fly a jet and combat swim: they were basic requirements for the royal heirs of Hellenia.

She wondered if that would pique his interest; he was a man of action after all. How would he take it if he knew that both she and Max, whom he saw as pampered royals, could do all he did and then some?

Charlie grinned. 'Are you going to bring me to the mat? Want to know how many ways I could take you down, princess?'

She shook herself. This half-sexual banter put her in a ridiculous situation; it was beneath her. 'We've just come out of ten years of civil war. There were ten million people in Hellenia fifteen years ago. We're down to eight million. Lord Orakis tends to eliminate competition in violent ways, and you and I both stand in his way. The king doubled the protection of all the royal family three years ago.' *After the palace attack.* And she intended to change the over-the-top protection levels, too, if—when—she became queen. He had to listen to her. He had to.

Charlie's brows lifted again, and she guessed he was digesting another facet to his unwanted elevation in status.

She sat down. 'We should get comfortable. There are things you need to know.'

'Shake out the list, it's miles long.' His tone was as dry as new wine as he sat opposite her. It seemed he was a man who liked his personal distance. 'We might need to ask the goons to bring in dinner and breakfast while they're out there doing nothing.'

The words made her hesitate; he was already on edge, and obviously didn't want to belong here. She abandoned her original, perhaps too harsh, words. 'Life is very different here—'

He laughed, hard-edged. Words couldn't adequately describe the wealth of half-repressed emotions it held.

Trying again, she forced herself to hold to her resolve. He'd been here less than an hour and he'd been threatened, had been given veiled bribes, and told he had no rights. A man like Charlie was bound to react badly to that. 'No doubt you've been brought up very differently to those of us within the royal family, but you're no longer in Australia.'

'Gee, thanks, Dorothy. If I could find my red shoes I'd disappear back to my life and career, and make everyone's lives easier.' He cocked his very handsome head back in the general direction of the door. 'His Furious Majesty's less than impressed with the new heir.'

Strange that his speech sounded so arrogant, yet she heard rough exhaustion, and his acceptance that Grandfather was right to be unimpressed. 'I'm trying to help you, but you're not making it easy,' she said, repressing the urge to grit her teeth.

At once his face and deep, velvety eyes softened, and again Jazmine felt that odd loss of emotional equilibrium. She felt less princess, and more...

'I'm sorry, princess. I'm sure you're as unhappy with this situation as I am.' He swept a hand over the suit. 'Even in the borrowed threads, I'm nobody's idea of a prince. Believe me, I know. I've had enough ex-girlfriends informing me of the fact.'

*Oh, but you could be*, she almost said, but he was obviously uncomfortable in his new skin. Showing him possibilities, or ordering him around, it would be alienation to him.

*No, just alien. He can't be expected to see life as I've been bred to do.*

Charlie had grown up ignorant of his heritage, in a modest four-bedroom brick home he'd occupied with his sister and friend until two days ago. Instead of years of royal training and sterling education at an international school and Oxford, or perhaps Yale or Harvard, he'd gone to a local high-school and had gone into fireman and para-medic training. He was a Marandis only in name. No, in Charlie's mind, he was a fireman from the backblocks of Sydney. He'd had no time to adjust, saw no reason *to* adjust.

Grandfather had made a tactical error in his peremptory summons and enforced extraditions of this pair. He expected Charlie to obey orders he didn't understand, to see his expected future as an honour, and accept his position when he had no idea what that future and position entailed. He'd made a mistake in expecting Charlie to bow to the royal will without full knowledge of *why* he and Lia were so necessary to the continuation of the Marandis royal family.

And, to Jazmine's mind, wanting him to be a traditional Marandis was as impractical as it was counterproductive to the future she had planned.

'Do you mind?'

Startled out of her plans, she looked at the cause of her hope and confusion. He'd shrugged off his jacket, and was tugging at his tie.

To her surprise, she smiled. 'Only if I can take off these heels. You have no idea how much they hurt after a couple of hours' standing.'

He grinned. 'Go for it. I won't tell.' He tugged at his tie and pulled it off, then undid the top three buttons on his shirt, and rolled up his sleeves. 'Hasn't this place got air-conditioning?'

'This house is almost four hundred years old.' Charlie's untamed golden masculinity, exposed in the open column of his shirt, emptied her head of everything but the need to stare her fill; to cover her pounding heart she added with would-be calmness, 'The real palace does, but we haven't lived there in a few years. It's still being repaired.' She half-expected him to ask why it was taking so long, or make a caustic comment on spoiled royals wanting everything perfect.

Instead, he said gently, 'I'm sorry.'

Confused again, she lifted her brows in query.

He smiled at her. 'Lady Eleni told us about the palace fire-attack during the war, and your father's and brother's deaths so soon after the war ended. It's no wonder you agreed to this engagement. Security's not to be sneezed at after all you've been through.'

Moved yet unnerved by kindness from a stranger, she turned her face. 'I barely knew my father or brother.' She willed control against the vast sorrow that there wasn't time to know Father or Angelo now. She turned back, forcing a smile. 'I was sent to school in Geneva when I was eight, and then attended finishing school. I was at university in London when I became Princess Royal, and summoned home. Father was busy with his duties, as was Angelo. I'd only been back here a year or two when they—' Without warning, her throat thickened. *Control, control!*

'I see,' he said very quietly.

She closed her eyes, struggling to go on.

He leaned forward and touched her hand. 'Lia and I lost our parents when I was seventeen. We'd all lived together, all three generations, all our lives, and Yiayia and Papou were fantastic, but...' He smiled at her. 'It's okay to cry sometimes, princess. I know I did my share when I felt so alone I could scream.'

The words were beautiful and foreign to everything she'd been raised to believe. *Don't cry, Jazmine,* her father had said at Mother's funeral, when she was seven. *You are a Marandis. You are strong!*

Her spine straightened. 'I'm sure you're right.'

The kindness and warmth vanished from his face. 'Sorry; I crossed the royal line. There's proof that I'm not a real prince, and I never will be.'

'But you are,' she said softly, backtracking fast, and letting the fact click into place: *he doesn't like being locked out.* 'Like it or not, you're a Marandis, Charlie, and we need to discuss—'

'Mmm. Say my name like that, and I'll discuss whatever you want.' A smile curved his mouth. 'Char-r-r-lie,' he said, as softly as she had, but with far more sensual intent. 'I never heard the Mediterranean burr in quite that way before. Your voice is so blurry and sexy. I love listening to you, Jazmine.'

And his eyes, lingering on her face, said, *and I really like looking at you.*

He spoke her name as it had been pronounced: *Zhahz-meen*. One word, just a name she'd heard ten-thousand times, but he'd turned it into silk and shadows, with the summery sensuality of a lush Arabian night.

Without warning, a new kind of wolf had leaped from his lair; the hidden lion was pouncing. He'd spoken to her not as princess, but as man to woman. And she felt the slow melt inside, feminine liquidity racing like quicksilver through her body. He'd taken her from blue-blooded princess to red-blooded woman with just a few soft words.

She'd never met a man like him before. He was unique, an unexpected prince in a fireman's skin, all hot-blooded male. He'd never learned to hide his emotions as she had. And, by his words, the look in his eyes and the slow burn in his touch, he wanted her to know he found her attractive. He didn't play diplomatic games; he didn't know how. This golden-skinned, dark-eyed man, strong and beautiful, a hero as much as any from the pages of *The Odyssey*, found her as attractive as she found him.

'And, as regards this engagement, it's a farce. I don't want to be here, and the last thing you need is a man who'll never fit into your world. Nobody can force us into this kind of thing in the twenty-first century. I swear on my life I'll get you out of this.'

She started out of her lovely daydream as his words sank in. And her heart sank right down with it.

# CHAPTER THREE

CHARLIE saw the instant distress in her eyes—
the intense disappointment—before something
clicked back into place, and the warm woman
she'd been became the 'Mona Lisa princess' the
tabloids called her: picture-perfect and smiling,
comfortable in the public eye, if remote somehow. 'What makes you assume I want to get out
of this?'

He stared, wondering if someone as lovely as
the princess could have only half her marbles. 'It
has to be obvious. Even a real-life princess must
want the whole nine-yard cliché: the handsome
prince, babies, a palace—and a happily-ever-
after. It's only by accident of birth I'm here. I'm
a Sydney boy, a rough-mannered fireman. I don't
have class, I don't do "for ever"—and I'm certainly not the guy who'd make your life easier.
I'm not what you'd call easy-going.'

Her smile grew, but it wasn't one he liked. It

made him feel out of control, and that was a feeling with which he was neither familiar nor comfortable. 'It seems I have at least six of those yards, Your Highness. A palace—' she waved her hand around '—and, if we married, babies would be part of the deal, I'd assume.'

His heart darkened at the thought of it. Royal children with royal minders, who'd have to bow and scrape to His Majesty's every whim? Not on his life. 'Four-and-a-half yards aren't enough for a woman like you.'

'I hadn't finished,' she said softly. 'In my opinion, I have a handsome prince, even if he's a reluctant one.' She broke the smugness with a bitten-lip grin, the woman in her peeping out for a moment, and he found himself responding in kind. 'If I must marry, I'd rather have a firecracker than a dog rolling over on order. You have a mind of your own, ideals and dreams. I respect that.'

Damn. Much as he liked her words—she'd made it obvious she found him attractive, and liked both his temper and his independence—now he had to be blunt. 'As tempting as you are, I don't want to get married, princess. I could *never* become what you'd want in a prince. I couldn't stand the constant intrusions into my life you endure from the press every day. It was bad enough after the fire a few months back, but if I had to handle it on a daily basis I'd end up hitting someone. Not very royal behaviour, is it?'

She shook her head, still smiling. 'I noticed your discomfort with the press—it was obvious in every photo. But, rest assured, we'd help you to acclimatise to that sort of thing.'

His jaw clenched tighter. 'I don't *want* to acclimatise,' he said baldly. 'I can't think of a single benefit in being here. I want to live my life without black-suited goons following me and cameras waiting for every stuff-up I make—and I *will* make them.'

Jazmine nodded, as if she'd expected him to say it. He found himself wondering what it would take to rattle her cage, to put a crack in her perfect composure. 'You do realize that the only way you can go home is by repudiating your position, which likely means your sister will go home with you?'

He shrugged. 'I don't see a problem with that. Lia likes her life at home.'

Her voice filled with gentle amusement. 'Have you asked Lia what she wants, or are you taking it for granted you can make a decision of this calibre for her?'

He felt his jaw clench. 'I know my sister. She's happy living with Toby and me, running her business and teaching the kids.' *Well, happy enough now*, he amended silently. After her failed attempt to enter the Australian Ballet on the heels of their parents' death in a car crash, it had brought on her dance with death-dealing anorexia. If it hadn't been for Toby's complete devotion to her returning to health—staying at the clinic with her day and night around their fire-fighting training-schedule—she might not have made it. Toby wasn't only the best friend he'd ever had, the brother he'd always wanted, he was the only person Lia trusted with her secrets.

Suddenly he wanted to hear Toby's voice saying everything would be okay, he'd be there soon, though it was sure to be said in four-syllable words he favoured. 'Lord of the Dictionary' Toby might be, but he was the staunchest, truest friend he and Lia could ever have.

There hadn't been any joking camaraderie or long words when they'd talked to him from the Consulate in Canberra. Toby's silent reaction to their sudden disappearance 'on family business', unable to say when they'd be home, unable to call again—unable even to talk it through with him as a result of the officials listening in on every word—had been an almost more frightening reality than the jet they'd been about to board. He,

Lia and Toby were family. None of the three of them had ever kept secrets from each other, as far as he knew.

Now he and Lia *were* secrets. Secrets of state. And he hadn't felt this alone since his parents' death.

'You know what your sister wants without asking her. I see.' The amusement lurking in Jazmine's eyes grew to an outright twinkle. She was so pretty, with that sparkle lighting her up from within. He'd always had a thing about that rich-chestnut colour, and she had it in a double dose: her eyes and hair. No wonder she was known as the last single beautiful princess in Europe, feted and courted by all the noble bachelors within five-thousand kilometres.

*I could be the one kissing her next. I could take her to bed in a matter of weeks...*

And thinking about that, looking into that face, suddenly the whole prince-and-arranged-marriage gig didn't seem so bad. The perks of unexpected royalty had never come in a more tempting package than Jazmine Marandis.

He dragged himself out of those thoughts before they turned dangerous. What had she been saying? Seeing something... 'You see what?' he demanded.

'I see why you and my grandfather clash. You both believe you know what's best for others without asking what they want. You're more of a Marandis than you realize.' Jazmine's infuriating half-smile grew. 'So you know she doesn't want to be a princess, live in the palace, marry a young and handsome Grand Duke— Oh, and inherit the fifty million euros that is her inheritance and dowry from the duchy?'

*Fifty million euros?* Charlie felt a cold shiver run down his back. Good God. He hadn't thought about the money; he'd been too furious to think. He'd concentrated on what *he* would lose, what *he* wanted.

What about Lia? Would she want the money, the lifestyle, the whole thing? What if she was attracted to the Grand Duke? Would Charlie ruin everything for her because *he* wanted to return to his life?

As if tapping into his thoughts, Jazmine asked conversationally, 'Have you always made decisions for Lia? I hear she runs a successful ballet school. Do you decide what concerts she'll do, check the accounts, or help her run it?'

'Of course not,' he snapped, hating that she was right. He had no right to decide for Lia. And he was really irritated that the snooty princess was holding all the cards. He knew nothing of this country, his new family or the laws. The only power he had was his independence. His 'pig-headed pride', as Lia put it.

He grinned suddenly, thinking of his sister as Princess Lia. Just as well his name wasn't Luke, or this whole thing really would have been a farce.

But, much as he hated to admit it, the 'Mona-Lisa princess' sitting across from him was correct. The title suited her, he thought sourly, with her intriguing, frustrating little smile, and eyes that saw too much. He had no right to decide the future for Lia. His shy, family-loving, homebody sister might hanker after the fairy-tale ending most women dreamed of, and after every-thing she'd been through she deserved it.

'What do you want from me?' he growled, backed into a corner for Lia's sake.

As if knowing she'd boxed him in, her smile turned hopeful. 'I only want you to give this life a chance before you disappear. And, please, stop trying to be my white knight. If you're no prince, I'm no damsel in distress.'

He felt the flush creeping up his neck. She was right. The fireman in him had crossed the world to a new kind of burning building, ready to carry out the helpless female trapped in a situation not of her making...or liking.

The muscles on her face didn't move, but he

knew she was smiling inside. That mysterious twinkle in her eyes, lurking deep, fascinated him with her unspoken secrets.

'And?' He could tell there was more.

'There's more at stake than your privacy, independence and pride, Charlie. Lives hang in the balance.' She leaned forward in earnest entreaty as she said his name again, and a hint of soft cleavage showed through the correct folds of her silky blouse.

Was her skin as silky-soft? Would she say his name with that sweet, sexy little burr as he slipped that blouse from her shoulders and down…?

*Shove it, jerk. She's a princess. With her minders, there's no chance of touching her before the wedding night. And a wedding night—or a wedding—just isn't happening!*

The only reason he was listening to her was because he didn't know what Lia wanted. He knew what *he* wanted. And that wasn't about to change, no matter how pretty and appealing the princess was. Because she *was* a princess, she came with her own set of royal chains, and he wasn't the guy to slip his wrists into the king's cuffs for any amount of money or power. She was bred to this life. He was here by accident of birth.

'So whose life is at stake?' He was proud of the even tone. Control established.

She frowned, her head tilting a little. 'You don't want to know what your inheritance is?'

For a moment he was tempted. Then the realization came: she'd only asked to weaken his resolve, to appeal to his greed—and when that didn't work no doubt she'd try another tack. She'd keep gently chipping away at his walls until, deprived of a safe perch, he'd fall off. And, like Humpty Dumpty, if he fell no amount of king's horses or men would put his life back the way it had been.

Surely she'd seen enough of him to know the only good he could do this place was to get back on that jet and return to his anonymous life in Sydney? If he hadn't even been able to help his own sister through anorexia, how the hell could he run a country?

'No, thanks,' he said abruptly. 'If I can't take it home with me, there's no point. So, what are the stakes? Whose lives "hang in the balance", as you put it so eloquently?'

She'd bitten her lip as he spoke—not on the outside, no, that wouldn't be classy enough for the perfect princess. But she'd worried the inside of her lip, and for some reason he couldn't fathom he found the act touching...sweet, and somehow lonely.

When she spoke, it was with a kind of desperate resolve. 'The lives and future of the people of Hellenia. Lasting peace in our nation.'

His brows lifted. 'All that depends on me?' he mocked, to cover the fact that he had the same sinking feeling in his gut he felt when he saw a fire gone beyond his ability to extinguish it.

'Yes.' Her eyes grew soft with pleading. 'Grandfather seems almost immortal, but he's eighty-two, and he's had two heart attacks already. If he dies without naming a male heir, it will mean disaster for Hellenia. It's obvious you believe you're the wrong man for the job, Charlie.' His body heated up again, hearing the blurry way she said his name. 'But don't judge Hellenia's needs or your suitability until you know our history. Being one of the few absolute monarchies left in the world—'

Before she could finish the State of the Nation address, she appeared to think better of it; her voice dropped, and turned husky with emotion. 'There's been such suffering in our country since your grandfather left. It can end with us.' Her words held entreaty and conviction—no longer the Princess dolly, but showing a bare hint of the passionate woman he'd seen before, and it fascinated him. 'This is bigger than us, what we want.'

With control still in place, his jaw didn't drop, but the shock lingered inside him, roiling his gut. 'Are you saying you *want* this crazy marriage?'

'Alliance,' she corrected, her eyes calm. 'Don't panic, Charlie; it isn't personal.' She nibbled the inside of her lip again. A subtle gesture, and one most wouldn't see, but Charlie could feel her fear, sense her worry, the loneliness of her position—and the stakes he still didn't know became more urgent, reflected in the shadows inside her eyes. Eyes that, looking more closely, he noted were more like old Irish whisky than chestnut. 'I know you care about others, or you wouldn't have risked your life for that little girl, or the dozens of others we discovered you've rescued.' Her gaze searched his in deep-hidden pleading and anxiety.

Not knowing what to say or do, he nodded, wishing he didn't have to, but her complete honesty demanded his in return.

'We need your help on a larger and more lasting scale than anyone you've saved in the past. There are five-hundred-year-old laws that need changing. Not merely that, but thousands of people lost family and homes and rights during the civil war. Some of my people have nothing. And, if you leave, they'll have nothing to look forward to. Nothing.'

Though she'd said it three times, the word still held a starkness, a rawness too strong for her to be putting on an act.

'I'm listening,' he said quietly.

Her eyes lit from within, and his body tightened in spite of the gravity of the conversation. She was so *pretty*, so certain of her convictions. 'I want to bring Hellenia into the modern world, but with the way the law currently stands I can't do it alone. If you renounce your position, I lose my chance. According to laws in place since we took power in the 1700s, there must be an heir from the male Marandis line, or the crown reverts to a direct descendant of the royal family that was forcibly removed in the 1700s. The Orakis family was deposed by the people for their selfish and immoral ways. The head of the rebel force—a national hero, Angelis Marandis—was asked to become king. Marandis didn't want to take the crown, but he did, for the sake of his people.'

Charlie nodded again, feeling an unwanted kinship with this long-dead relative. He'd heard most of this from the ambassador in Canberra, but it was obvious she had something to say, and interrupting her would break her train of thought.

The princess sighed. 'The Orakis family never left. They've started civil wars, fomented unrest in troubled times—such as during World War Two, when our ally Greece was overrun. The troubles in Albania have given the Orakis supporters the opportunity to try to regain power in secret during the last twenty years.' She stopped, nibbling her lip again. Looking almost adorably lost.

Trying with all his might not to respond to her plea, to touch her, he nodded. 'Lady Eleni told us all that in Canberra.'

She smiled at his awkward attempt to comfort her. 'Sorry if I appear to be going over old ground, but you need to understand why your decision is important to far more people than you and Lia. Markus Orakis is an autocrat in the old mould, believing in his right to rule. Orakis's father spent twenty years trying to reclaim the throne.' She blinked once, twice, but the suspicious sheen turned her eyes into beautiful mirror-pools of the suffering she saw in her people's future. She looked up, those mysterious eyes shimmering with emotion, drenching his soul with her courage and her selfless duty.

'It's not that he's a terrorist—he's not. He just wouldn't *change* anything. He'd keep Hellenia in the seventeenth century to keep the monarchy absolute and unchallenged. He'd put his family and followers in strategic positions to consolidate his power, and destroy anyone who threatened him.' She sighed. 'You've watched the international news, right? This isn't melodrama. It's what this kind of man *does*. They start with good intentions, doing good to the nation, then power goes to their heads and they justify any act of violence. He's already that way with the following he has.'

Again, Charlie nodded. Anyone who watched the news could name the dictators who'd done exactly as Jazmine was predicting Orakis would do. 'Go on.'

She touched his hand, and he could feel her trembling as she delivered her final words with the subtlety of a battle axe to his skull. 'Ask yourself—if he could have returned, would your grandfather have done so? For his people, the people he loved? And, now he can't, wouldn't he want you and Lia to try?'

*Ah, hell...*

*Click:* a tiny sound in his brain, but deadly. It was the sound of manacles around his wrists. She'd found the key to his capitulation, and turned it without hesitation.

If he could have, Papou *would* have come back. He'd have urged Charlie to try to help if he could—and, despite his denial, he knew Lia's answer. In all her life she'd never let anyone down, never said no if she was in a position to help. To her, the suffering in Hellenia would make this choice a sacred commission, the chance to put right Papou's wrong in choosing love over duty.

An hour into their relationship, and she'd put his wrists in cuffs. For the sake of the Hellenican people: Papou's people; her people. And for *her* sake, because it seemed the perfect princess did need a hero after all.

The perfect shell of the mysterious princess was a fragile illusion that, when shattered, couldn't be reinstated. Those private, proud eyes had cried for him, and if he turned his back now he'd regret it for the rest of his life.

'Enough, Your Highness.' His tone froze even him, but he was losing the freedom he treasured. He might have to accept it, but he didn't have to like it. 'I'll go back in there and behave. I gather that's what you want?'

The appealing loveliness of her vanished as if it had never been. 'There will be much more than that, Your Highness—but let's take on one obstacle at a time.'

She was every inch the princess, cool and detached. But the woman of passion and commitment lingered like a super-imposition; her warm and vital heart beat beneath the icy layer she projected. He saw the princess, but heard the woman within. He saw her, beautiful and so earnest, pleading with him to stay. She'd stripped her defences, not for herself, but for the sake of her people.

He wondered why, when she could have used other cool, level-headed arguments, she'd chosen to show her real, hidden self to him.

'Time to bow to the old dragon,' he said, not without ruefulness. He didn't want to, but he'd given his word. He put the choking tie back in place as she slipped her feet back into the heels that were way too high for so small a woman. 'See, princess, I can pretend to be civilized every now and then.'

The smile she gave in return seemed remote, yet the super-imposition remained. As if she stood in a mirror, he could see the reflection of her uncertainty beneath—and it was that hidden woman under the princess's surface face he couldn't make himself reject.

He held out his arm to her. He'd have liked a more intimate touch. Holding hands would tell him if the simmering fascination he was feeling for her was returned, or if it was all duty on her side.

But the minders waited on the other side of the

door. And two stood in strategic positions outside on the terrace. When it came to private matters, he'd never been one to put on a show.

Jazmine rose gracefully to her feet and slipped her arm through his. 'Think of it as a game,' she suggested. 'You say yes, you capitulate—for now—and you make plans. When it's your turn, you can change what you like, from law, protection levels and privacy, to the rate of taxes.'

He felt his brows lift. 'Very clever, Your Highness.'

She inclined her head, but not before he caught the twitching grin, the tiny quiver of a half-dimple at the side of her mouth, and the lurking mischief in her eyes.

He knew he'd remember her face, caught in that moment in time, for the rest of his life. The superior Mona Lisa: dutiful princess, a passionate, committed woman and a sweet tease all in one. And she was beautiful like this, so beautiful.

The door opened as they approached. He flicked a glance around, and saw the security cameras in every corner.

Strangers had been watching his every move, listening to every private word between himself and Jazmine. Like it or not, he *had* been putting on a show.

It would be that way for the rest of his life, if he took this on. There would be no treasured private moments between husband and wife. Every sound would be noted by the security outside, even if there were no hidden cameras.

This wasn't the start of something between a man and a woman, it was a farce, a half-tragic sitcom for the edification of a legion of strangers.

He wanted to puke, to bolt back to that big silver jet and head back to a life where he didn't have people watching, a king telling him what to do, and a princess who made him feel like a jerk and a hero at the same time.

'I know this life is difficult, but I have one tenet I live by: nobody can take away my dignity—not a camera, a king, or a nation,' she whispered, close to his ear, so the minders wouldn't hear. 'Only I can do that…if I allow it.'

Her breath touched his ear, fluttered over the skin of his neck. His sense of danger went on full alert. Her Royal Highness Princess Jazmine was like no woman he'd ever known. Beneath the cool, sweet smile he'd seen in a hundred captions, she was her own woman, unique and private.

She hadn't been forced to give a treasured part of herself to him; she'd come willingly, warm as summer, and then as cool as an autumn breeze.

Who was this woman? It wasn't her beauty drawing him, though heaven knew her face haunted him already. Something in her called him. He knew whatever came, if he walked, she wouldn't be a bland memory. She was light and dark, heaven and hell, and had made him feel all of them at once in a half-hour time period.

All the passion beneath the smiling façade, the unashamed love for others, the devotion to duty, found an echo inside his soul.

He wanted to help her—he wanted to see that impish grin, the shimmering glow in her eyes. He wanted to be the hero she needed. He wanted... Oh, damn, he just *wanted*—and that scared the living daylights out of him. Even with the protection and cameras and media speculation, Jazmine wasn't a woman a man could walk away from—and he didn't mean the princess. Would she be the one he'd never forget...or always regret? Or the price he'd have to pay for wanting to play the hero?

# CHAPTER FOUR

'YOU want me to *what*? No. Absolutely not.'

Oh, help…

Until now, Charlie had behaved impeccably with the king. He'd apologized for his earlier rudeness, and had listened to the old man's dictums with surprising patience, asking intelligent questions, showing a willingness to think about the sudden one-eighty his life had taken, and the reasons why he should try 'this prince caper', as he'd called it.

Jazmine stifled a grin at the memory of the king's thinly disguised shock at the terminology this irreverent royal had used.

'The rumours are already circulating, Kyriacou,' the king replied to Charlie's flat refusal with a calm Jazmine knew he was far from feeling. 'We need to make an announcement to the press regarding your presence here. We need to introduce you to the media, and your future people, as soon as possible.'

'And make another one when I humiliate the royal family, or the press-chases freak me out to the point where I decide not to take it on?' Charlie's voice was rich with a delicious kind of self-irony. 'You wouldn't make a fool of yourself and your government that way.'

'Not if you stay—and not if you take the lessons you'll receive to heart.'

Charlie's brow lifted at the command in the king's tone. 'Whether I do either will remain my choice, with all due respect, sire. I won't agree to anything until I have full knowledge of what life will be like for Lia and myself as...*royals*.'

The distaste in the emphasis he used couldn't be missed. The truth was obvious to everyone: he was here only under sufferance.

His sufferance, or hers?

Jazmine worried the inside of her cheek. Had she gone too far with her plea? Until now, she'd been prepared to do whatever it took to make him stay—but Charlie was no tame canary who'd enjoy the press attention and all the trappings of this life. They might be surrounded by luxury, but all Charlie saw was the cage beneath the shining gold...and that perception was something only he could change, because, no matter how she painted it, he was right: the cage existed.

She'd had no choice but to make him aware that the stakes were higher than he knew, but if she was forcing him into life here—a life that included *her*—by guilt...

Faced with the handsome, freedom-loving reality of the new prince, Jazmine's songs of noble self-sacrifice had had a background melody of handcuffs and chains. But the consequences of his possible desertion were too devastating—both to the nation and to the woman.

'Sire, if I might speak, Charlie and I both are coming to know what's at stake. We've listened to you, and we understand why our decision is so important,' Lia said, looking earnestly into the king's eyes. 'Charlie's never walked away from something he believed to be his duty, or refused to help when he could. Papou followed the news here. I believe he saw this day coming. He taught us that it's a sacred duty to help others whenever we can.'

She smiled at Charlie. Jazmine saw his face turn wry with self-mockery, and the loving resignation that, yes, she'd painted their grandfather with a perfect brush. And she found that fascinating. Why had the Grand Duke trained his grandchildren for royal life, but never returned himself?

'Yeah, but *he* didn't come back and do the job he'd been trained for, did he?' Charlie muttered, echoing Jazmine's thoughts so perfectly she felt as if he'd reached in and plucked them from her head.

'Maybe he felt he was no longer worthy enough—or wouldn't be welcome,' she suggested softly, and Charlie winced.

After checking to see if Jazmine had any more to say, Lia continued speaking to the king. 'There's a lot of what ifs and maybes in this for us all, sire. We need to know if we can handle our duties, and you need to know that too. So you must allow us both some time to make the right decision—both for the nation, and for us.'

'There's no *must* about it, girl,' the king snapped, but his eyes were soft with an affection Lia seemed to inspire in everyone she met, even in crabbed old men used to their own way.

Jazmine looked at Lia through new eyes. Yes, she'd be perfect here. A sleepy-eyed beauty with an obvious sense of duty, integrity, natural humility and the adorable factor: Lia had the potential to become a magnificent princess, beloved by the people, the press and the family.

Jazmine's belief in her was proven moments later, by Grandfather's warm, almost loving words—spoken with a feeling *she'd* often wished to receive from him. 'You're right, Giulia. I need to know you're able to handle your responsibilities with the necessary dignity and courage. So far I have little doubt about you.' His tossed glance at Charlie made him look far colder than he really was. 'I agree your brother needs time— and training.'

Jazmine wondered about the hidden family dynamics that had led to Grandfather's judging Charlie so harshly, based on Charlie's natural enough reluctance to change his life without warning, but had given in so freely to Lia…

'At least we agree on something.' Charlie moved as if to rise, then seemed to think better of it. 'Your Majesty, I came off a four-day shift to this news, and flew straight here. I never sleep well on planes, even first-class jets.' With an effort, he smiled. 'I assume you've had rooms prepared for us?'

'Of course, Kyriacou.' The effort to smile back was palpable, but Grandfather did it. 'Jazmine will show you to your rooms in the east wing. Giulia, I assume you would also like to rest? Max will show you the way to your rooms. They're in the west wing.'

For the first time, Lia frowned. 'Sire, I prefer to have rooms close to Charlie.'

The king stared at her from behind his glasses. 'That's not possible.'

Charlie put an arm around Lia's shoulder. 'You're the king, aren't you? Make it possible,' he said with blunt aggression.

'You don't understand. Segregation of the sexes is an accepted fact for royalty unless it's a married couple. It's been this way for centuries. The people expect it.'

Charlie hugged Lia closer. 'No, *you* don't understand. Lia and I aren't royal—yet—and if you don't make this happen we never will be.'

'No, it's all right, Charlie. I'm sorry to have started this fuss.' Lia hugged Charlie before stepping away from him, standing with quiet pride as she smiled at the king. 'We've always lived together, and he's all the family I have left.'

Jazmine saw a shadow pass in Charlie's self-contained eyes, and, having read the files on their past, realized why he'd untied the fragile accord between himself and the king. But Lia had shown a quiet strength that made Jazmine want to hug her, to cheer. Yes, she'd be a magnificent princess…if the life didn't send her screaming for home.

The realization made her speak. 'The people couldn't possibly be offended at a brother and sister being close, Grandfather. If I give my room to Charlie, no one needs to know. Nobody else shares my wing, and none of the staff would dare

gossip if you endorsed the order.' She saw the ire
in her grandfather's wily eyes, and knew she'd be
hearing his opinion on her rebellion later. And
that was fine with her. She had some questions for
him, too. 'My room's beside yours,' she said,
turning to smile at Lia. 'I can move into the suite
a floor up.'

'Thank you for the offer, Jazmine. But, truly,
I'll be fine. Living next to you will be fun.'
Gratitude and impish fun shimmered in Lia's
slumberous eyes, and Jazmine knew she'd made
a friend for life.

Charlie didn't speak, just smiled at Jazmine—
and the power of his deep-hidden relief and warm
gratitude made her feel as if she'd tumbled down
a flight of stairs: winded, unsure of her standing
and her dignity.

Inexplicably she wanted to see it again, to see
the warm approval and thanks in those liquid dark
eyes, even if she did find it hard to breathe. Even
if she did fall.

'I'll show you to your rooms.' *Charlie's room.*
She found herself blushing, which was ridiculous. Lia had risen to the occasion—it wasn't as
if he was going to…

*Sleep in my bed.*

The thought leaped into his eyes at the same

moment. Fire met heat in eyes unable to look away from each other. Her throat closed up, her pulse pounded.

Oh, could she be any more pathetic? A quick glance showed Max and Lia studiously weren't looking, Grandfather's face was smug...and Charlie was hiding a grin. Why didn't she make a formal press release? *I find the new Crown Prince of Hellenia more than passingly attractive.*

Charlie swept his free hand out. 'Lead the way, princess. Feel free to come along, Your Grace,' he added to Max, with the mocking note that told Jazmine Charlie wouldn't consider belonging here.

'Lia, will you walk with me?' she offered on impulse. Brother and sister were obviously an unbreakable entity—but Lia had proved to have a stronger will than Charlie suspected. If she could get to know Lia, to make her see the importance of their decision, how much she could do for this country and the people.

Lia smiled. 'I'd love to.' She gently detached herself from Charlie's grip, and slipped her arm through Jazmine's. 'I don't suppose we can order hot chocolate and popcorn? I'd love to have a really good "getting to know you" talk.'

Remembering the blip in Lia's past, and the hard anxiety in Charlie's eyes whenever he spoke of or for his sister, Jazmine grinned. 'I've been outnumbered by the men for far too long. Some fun food and cosy girl-talk is exactly what I need.'

Though she wasn't looking at him, she felt the tension in Charlie's body unwind, like a taut spring held too long. She felt the warmth of his unspoken gratitude touching her right down to her soul.

She just…felt him.

'It seems the girls will have their way.' The king chuckled and rose to his feet. 'Max, you might want to take Kyriacou to his room. Maybe after a few hours' rest, you'll be ready for a tour of the house and gardens, or the city. It's a beautiful place, truly medieval in places.' He waved at Max and Jazmine. 'The cars along with drivers, or walking in the grounds and the forest, are at your disposal whenever you wish it.'

For the first time, Charlie smiled without restraint at Grandfather. 'Thank you, Your Majesty.' Jazmine could almost hear the unspoken question hovering on his lips: *if everyone's segregated, why are you asking Jazmine to show me to my room?*

The answer was embarrassing, no matter which way you looked at it. She wasn't about to volunteer the information. She'd never been one to thrust her head in a noose.

Jazmine walked with her arm in Lia's and chatted

about the portraits of their ancestors and the paintings lining the walls, from Constable to Pollock. She led the procession towards the stairs to the west wing with all her usual grace, and hoped no one else could see the unsteadiness in her legs, the trembling of her fingers. He was too close. Too hot-tempered. Too—just *too*. Too, too much.

Oh, why hadn't deportment lessons included ways to hide your emotions when you feel a sudden burst of desire as real and strong as this?

So the pretty princess did know he was a man, after all.

Remembering the blush, the half-hidden look in her eyes as she'd realized he could have been sleeping in her bed, Charlie grinned. Who'd have thought a guy from the backblocks of Ryde would get a hot look from royalty?

The answer was right in front of him, but he wouldn't look at it. He was Charlie Costa, the grand fighter of fires, the prince of rebels. Anything else was still too ridiculous to contemplate.

She was being so kind to Lia. She knew about the anorexia, and she seemed to be handling Lia almost as well as Toby could. Lia had been the one to ask about hot chocolate just when he'd started to worry. She hadn't had more than a cup of tea since arriving at the palace. Stressing inevitably led to a loss of appetite.

But Lia had asked for food, for girl-talk, was happy to be rooming beside Jazmine—Lia, who rarely spoke to strangers—and the warmth in the princess's answers made him remember the odd look of loneliness he'd seen earlier. Maybe Jazmine needed a friend as much as Lia did.

'Do you get the feeling we've been locked out?'

Hearing the vein of amusement in the Grand Duke's voice, Charlie grinned at him. 'Girls do that. It's part of their mystery and charm.'

'Yes, but two such handsome and refined personages as ourselves?'

He chuckled. 'You might be refined, Your Grace. I'm nothing of the kind.'

The Grand Duke smiled. 'Call me Max. We're cousins, even if it's rather distant…Charlie.'

He put out his hand. 'Don't you have a good Hellenican name like the rest of us?'

Max's eyes twinkled. 'I do, but if I told you then I'd have to kill you.'

Disarmed, Charlie laughed. 'It seems the men in this family have a thing about using their given names—*Max*.'

'And showing the truth inside their personalities.' Max shook his hand. 'You're a firecracker, but you're not half as vulgar as you'd like us to think you are.'

'Told you they'd see through it, Charlie,' Lia commented from ten feet ahead of them, her voice filled with laughter. 'You really don't scare anybody.'

'Speak for yourself,' Jazmine retorted. 'He makes *me* nervous.'

Lia chuckled. 'I don't blame you. I love my brother, but I wouldn't want to have to even *think* about marrying him.'

Jazmine gasped, and a smothered giggle emerged.

Max chuckled. 'Never assume a woman isn't listening, even when she's talking.'

'Damn multi-tasking,' Charlie grumbled, and the women laughed again as he'd hoped they would.

It was a sound he hadn't heard enough of from his sister in the past decade, unless she'd been with Toby. His sister was so private, too self-contained. She'd been that way since their parents had died. She must really have connected to Jazmine.

But Lia had constantly amazed him since this nightmare had begun. She'd handled their sudden elevation in life and crossing the world, the shocking proposition before them, living at the other end of this massive palace from her only family, with more courage and good sense than even he'd expected from her. She'd shown only strength and grace in the past thirty hours, while he was still reeling.

Yet he couldn't help worrying. If she became stressed, she'd stop eating. It was her measure of control when her world spun out of reach...and if that happened he wouldn't know what to do. He'd totally lost it when she'd collapsed.

Man, he wished Toby was here.

The Costas had never been the average Greek family, reliant on the wider Greek community for companionship and marriage mates. Now he knew why. Papou must have been worried his accent or something about him would lead to his being recognized.

So, while they'd had friends, both Greek and Australian, they'd mostly kept to themselves. They'd forged a tight little family unit—Mum and Dad, Yiayia and Papou, Lia, Charlie, and Toby, when a mutual fascination with firefighting cemented a careless acquaintance into unbreakable friendship. Toby's friendship had seen him through the worst years of his life.

Toby had a way with Lia too. He *knew* Lia, from her guarded heart to her deepest soul. Charlie's instinctive protectiveness was less comforting to Lia than Toby's cheerful grin, his careless hug or the suggestion that they bake something ridiculous or impossible. And, if that didn't work, he'd take her a ride on his motorbike into their beloved mountains for one of their four-hour hikes. She always came home happy, at peace with herself.

The princess opened a door, and motioned for Lia to precede her.

Another reason for Toby to be here was that then Charlie might find time to pursue the princess's budding interest in him. Though he'd been popular with the opposite sex since he was sixteen and had begun body training for entry into the Fire Brigade, there was something about Princess Jazmine he couldn't define—a deeper, elusive quality that told him she wasn't as she appeared.

'I know,' Max said softly.

Charlie started, realizing he'd been staring at Jazmine's swaying walk, her lovely peach of a bottom beneath the crisp linen skirt. He swung round to stare Max out.

Unintimidated, Max grinned. 'She doesn't know she does it to a man, but she does. The way she walks, she laughs— Well, all I can say is you're a lucky man.'

Charlie swung around fast, fists clenched. 'Then why the hell didn't you marry her while you could?' he said in an undertone.

Max shrugged. 'I've known her since she was a skinny stick with her hair in plaits, and she's known me since before my first pimple. We're like brother and sister. The engagement was hard on us both. The thought of taking her to bed just wasn't...' He grinned down at Charlie's fists. 'I beg your pardon for intruding.'

'You didn't intrude on anything except a dog-tired guy on shift too long.' He uncurled his hands, feeling like a jerk. 'Just show me to my room.'

Then Lia cried, 'Charlie!'

The utter delight in Lia's voice didn't stop the rush to her side, the panic that she'd get sick again if he wasn't there to protect her day and night. 'What is it, Lia?'

Lia was gazing around her new suite, her eyes wide. *'Oraio,'* she whispered: *superb, beautiful.* *'Now* I feel like a princess.'

Pulled outside his habitual worry, Charlie looked and blinked. *'Kita politeria,'* he muttered, using Papou's old expression of disgust: *is this where our taxes go?*

Jazmine laughed. 'You think this is luxurious? Wait until the palace renovations are complete. Then you'll have something to gape at. We each have our own wing there.'

'You're joking, right?' Charlie frowned, not least

because the rippling sound of her laugh still reso-
nated inside him, like the echo of a distant
memory, sweet and haunting. 'This one suite's
already as big as the house Lia and I have at home.'
For answer she winked, her dark lashed, malt-
whisky eyes shimmering with humour. 'Gotcha.'
Her tongue appeared between her teeth, not quite
poking out, just enough to be a cheeky challenge.
The half-dimple south-west of her mouth quivered.

Whatever else he'd expected of her, it wasn't in-
offensive jokes at his expense. He hadn't known
royals *could* tease.

A goddess in a silky, laughing package of woman;
Princess Jazmine was a bundle of sweet contradic-
tions. Nothing about her was as he'd expected, apart
from the lovely face he'd seen on magazine covers.
And everything he hadn't expected her to be was
all the things he'd always liked in a woman.

A bolt of lust shot right through him, so strong
it was almost painful—

And in front of his sister! His blood was so
hot it almost boiled, and for the one woman it
shouldn't, because, no matter how she twisted
his guts, he couldn't have her. She came with a
price tag way beyond anything he was willing to
pay. He was a fireman, not a prince, and that was
how it was going to stay.

Lust passed. Regrets didn't.

He wheeled around. 'Show me my room, will you, Max?'

He stalked through the door before the Grand Duke could answer.

# CHAPTER FIVE

WHY were five of them sitting at a table for over a dozen? Why did a 'family dinner', as the king had put it, feel like rehearsal for a State dinner?

As the fifth course made its way out, Charlie repressed a yawn. Pre-dinner wine, soup, palate refresher; dinner wine, salad, palate refresher. Now, after an hour, the main meal was about to arrive with a third glass of wine—and he was too wired up and exhausted to eat. He'd been starving when he'd walked in accompanied by Lia, the princess and the Grand Duke—but all this pomp and state left him so exhausted he could have fallen asleep on his exquisite napkin.

How many hours did he have before the month he'd agreed to this afternoon was over and he could go home? Home to his meat pies and chips for lunch, a beer at the local pub after a long day at work, and coming home—with Toby, most nights—to Lia's excellent home-cooking. The freedom to date a woman he liked, without the tabloids speculating when he'd marry her.

What more could an ordinary guy want from life?

But as much as he wanted to he said nothing, because again Lia was eating. She was basking in the king's grandfatherly attention and affection—the kind she'd missed so much since Papou had passed away last year. She was glowing under his tutelage, seeming to know instinctively which fork to use, how much wine to drink.

Unlike him. The king had snapped orders at him every thirty seconds, so many his fogged brain couldn't take them all in: "Sit up straight, Kyriacou… Smaller portions on the fork, boy… If you eat correctly there is no need to lean over your plate… You cannot leave the carrots uneaten; that is what children do, and will inspire no respect for you… One eats all the salad that is on the plate… One must *never* mash food together in that manner. It's what commoners do, not princes of the blood!"

*I am a commoner*, he'd wanted to retort. But for the sake of his promise to Jazmine he sat straight, ate smaller portions and filled his mouth with the despised carrots, without lettuce or cucumber with dressing to make them bearable. He chewed and swallowed over and over, hating the burst of fresh flavour every time he put another forkful in.

'You must show self-control. A royal personage must keep his head,' the king reproved coolly when he called for and received a second glass of dinner wine.

He counted to ten, tried to take another delicate mouthful of the sorbet, but he really couldn't repress it any longer. 'You mean the guillotine's still reserved for royals who don't pass the ceremonial-ritual meal test without using the wrong fork or running for the nearest anaesthetic?' he asked in tones of mock-horror, replacing the glass on the snowy tablecloth with unseemly haste.

He winked at Lia, who was trying hard not to laugh. He noticed Jazmine's pressed lips and dancing eyes, and Max's shoulders shaking, though his face was deadpan.

The king frowned. 'I am prepared to make allowances for your ignorance with the ways of royalty, Kyriacou, but if Giulia can manage with ease surely you can too? And there's no need to be facetious about instructions you certainly need.'

His fogged brain saw red at the deliberate rudeness, not even masked in humour. 'Believe me, Your Majesty, there is a need. If I don't laugh, I might end up jumping off the nearest balcony out of sheer boredom or fainting from hunger waiting to be fed,' he retorted, with a kind of weary politeness that sent the other three into fresh spasms of repressed laughter. 'I lost my appetite after the second round of green-and-white stuff. Where we come from, sorbet or ice cream is served as dessert, not after soup.'

The king sighed harshly. 'The *palate refresher* ensures you enjoy your meal.' The implication was clear: *and if you had any class, you'd know it.*

Charlie clamped his jaw shut.

'So tell us about your life in Australia,' Jazmine said in a gentle voice that in no way sounded like the intervention it was. 'It must be exciting to be a firefighter.'

'The sooner he forgets about that part of his life, the better,' the king decreed, his voice hard as ice.

The smile died on Charlie's face. He forgot why he was trying his best to keep quiet as his famous temper flashed to the surface. 'If yelling at me, illegally imprisoning me and forcing me to suffer through three-hour meals is the alternative you're offering to my life, Your Majesty, you'd better find a way to give me a dose of amnesia, because it's the only way I'll find living in Hellenia more attractive. My name is Charlie Costa, I am Australian, and I don't eat, walk or talk like one of you. If that's what you expect of me, you're going to fail.'

Something cold and dangerous glittered in the king's dark eyes. 'I do not fail, Kyriacou—and, from now on, you will not either.'

Charlie burst into laughter. 'You can't stop me, Your Majesty. I am who I am. You want Kyriacou Marandis, but I'm Charlie Costa, Australian fire-fighter, and there's nothing you can do to change it.'

Dead silence met his words. No one spoke for a full minute.

Then half a dozen servants entered the formal dining room with antique silver platters laden with all kinds of meats and vegetables.

Slowly he pushed his chair back. 'If you'll excuse me, I seem to be feeling nauseous. Must be the jet lag. I'm sure I'll be better able to face a twelve-course breakfast after a good night's sleep.'

Before the king could speak, Jazmine jumped in. If she didn't broker some form of peace between these two, the Costas would be gone before a week was out. *Why* was Grandfather being so hard on Charlie? He already seemed to dote on Lia. 'It's fine, Charlie. The past two days have been overwhelming, and you're exhausted.'

Even with the dark shadows beneath his eyes, the power of his smile knocked her sideways... Um, what had she been saying?

Lia said quietly, 'Thank you, Jazmine. I don't

think either of us slept this afternoon. If you'll excuse us...'

The king inclined his head with a smile. 'Of course, my dear. I should have thought of that. Sleep well.' He even flicked a small, tight smile Charlie's way. 'Good night, Kyriacou.'

As a concession, it was grudging; even to Jazmine it felt more like the Christmas détente on the Western Front than a cessation of hostilities. But, even exhausted, Charlie wasn't one to ignore a challenge. 'Good night, sire.' Spoken with respect, but he was standing his ground. Jazmine found her respect for him deepening.

Lia smiled and quietly left the room. Max was chatting to her as he accompanied her to her wing.

Which left Charlie to Jazmine, as Max had no doubt intended. Was he playing matchmaker, or throwing the fluttering pigeon to the dark, sleek, rebellious cat?

If she thought about it, she'd blush and stammer at all the stupid things she'd done this afternoon. She'd already embarrassed herself enough. She was supposed to be the one with poise and dignity.

'I'll show you to your room. It can be confusing for the first day or two.'

The look in his eyes told her she wasn't fooling

anyone, and, despite her will, that ridiculous blush was returning.

Once in the main hall, she turned to the silent minders. 'We don't need you now, thank you. We're not leaving the house.' They bowed and scattered.

Charlie's brows rose. 'You can do that?'

Still lost in her embarrassment, she answered honestly. 'I can when we're here, safe. In public I can direct them to certain tasks.'

'*You* can? Does that mean I can't wave my goons off?'

Jazmine wanted to sigh. What was it about this man that made her say more than she needed to? She'd always been so discreet…until this day of blunders and blurting. 'You will be able to once you've accepted your position.' She tried to say it calmly, with a positive direction. 'Once you've been trained to recognize the dangers and know when it's safe to be alone.'

'I've had years of that kind of training, princess. It's ingrained in me.'

'Right now you only know physical dangers, Charlie—a fire, falling roofs and walls, and the like. You haven't been through civil war, or lived in the crosshairs of a sniper's rifle.'

Finally Jazmine *did* close her eyes. Could she have said anything more calculated to send this over-protective brother straight back to safe Sydney?

'Things have been that bad here? For you, I mean?' he asked quietly.

Startled, she swung around to look at him. How did she balance truth with not scaring him all the way back Down Under? 'It's not only here in Hellenia, Charlie. Even peaceful nations surround their leaders with security. Every nation, every monarchy, democracy and totalitarian state has its enemies, and those who believe they should rule instead. We live in dangerous times, where "innocent until proven guilty" can mean people aren't held accountable for their actions, and weapons are freely available on the Internet.' She shrugged a little. 'When people think of royalty, they think of riches and limos, jets and tiaras, waving to an adoring crowd, and living in a palace. While we do have all that, the reality is far more complex.'

Even as she heard herself speak, she wanted to turn and thump her head against the wall. Could she have put it any worse? Did she *want* him to grab Lia and bolt to that jet as fast as he could?

'As the sole heir until now, you must have been surrounded by bullet-proof glass.'

It was said tentatively, like a question. She

nodded, relieved he'd looked at it from an outsider's point of view. For the first time she was glad he didn't see himself as royal. 'It has been rather restrictive since...' Again the unexpected lump rose in her throat. *Since I've been completely alone, apart from Grandfather, who expects duty and gives little or no affection...except to Lia.*

'I'm sorry, princess.' His voice was warm with compassion. 'I didn't mean to remind you of your loss.'

He touched her arm in awkward comfort. The strangest feeling streaked through her, like warm chills racing just under her skin, and then fear ran alongside those goosebumpy chills. If she reacted so strongly to one simple touch, she'd make a complete fool of herself if she ever found herself in his big, muscled, firefighter's arms.

'Thank you.' Two words, not quite clipped, but not letting him in. She had to find some distance from this man who'd turned her life upside down and inside out in a matter of hours.

The tenderness on his face vanished, and a tiny part of her rejoiced, because she'd seen that look on his face for Lia. Whatever else she was, she was *not* prepared for him to see her as a sister. 'I know my way from here, princess. Thanks for the guide.'

Now she really wanted to hit something. Where had the inborn diplomat in her gone? She'd always trodden the waters of people's emotions, walking the tightrope of royal distance and approachable warmth without sinking, but with Charlie she always seemed to overbalance. 'We need to talk.'

His brow lifted. 'No offence, princess, but I've been here eight hours, and in that time you've given me more than enough to think about. If you give me more, the silicon chip in my head will hit "overload".'

She couldn't blame him. Obviously it was time to back off a little, to give him space. 'I understand that, Charlie. But your lessons in royal behaviour and protocol will begin tomorrow.'

His laugh was filled with disbelief. 'You people really don't understand the meaning of the term jet lag, do you? I just finished a four-day shift with about a three-hour daily-sleep average. I fought five fires in that time, two of them major stuff. Two of my good friends are being treated in hospital. Do you think I'm always as reactive and rude as I've been today? Why do you think Lia's covering for me? I'm *tired*, princess.'

*You think you're tired? Try living a week as the only royal in a country torn by war and not enough funds to repair everything, travelling from one end of the nation to the other, meeting officials from everywhere to beg or borrow funds, and see how tired you are then!*

She had to grit her teeth again, and remind herself Charlie's reaction was normal, given that until yesterday he'd been a normal man. 'Of course, they'll start once you've slept,' she said, with a smile. That was it—show him some gracious capitulation while still making the boundaries clear, and maintain distance. Because, even though he was exhausted and halfway into shutdown, the dark heat of him, the fire he was keeping banked, was making the woman in her wake up.

All her life she'd been cool, reasoned, gentle and generous—everything she'd been expected to be. No man had given her more than an hour or two of wondering what it would be like to step outside her duty and become a real woman. She'd thought herself immune from physical desire, above what she'd been taught to believe was a mere human weakness. All her life she'd put her country first, as she ought to do.

All it had taken was one smile from a real man, one touch, to show her how human and utterly feminine she really was.

And how big-mouthed. Again. 'Grandfather

and I decided that it's best for now, given that you don't want to make any announcements, if I become your sole tutor in protocol for the next two or three weeks.'

Charlie turned at that, his brows furrowed in a deep frown. 'Protocol or seduction, Your Highness?' he drawled, the banked fury flaring up. 'Are all bets off here? Is this "let's get Charlie to agree at any cost"?'

She felt herself blushing. It was as if he'd been a fly on the wall in Grandfather's private rooms: *He might hate me, but I've seen the way he's looking at you, girl. Do the come-hither dance with him. Don't let him touch you, but make him think he could...* 'I'm to make certain you're ready for anything, from meeting the press to foreign diplomats, as well as basic flight-training.' It took a massive effort to speak as if he'd been wrong. 'There's a lot more to this job than you think.'

One of those frowning brows lifted. 'Flight training?'

She nodded, relieved he'd taken the bait. 'Once you've decided to stay—' *That's it, Jazmine, sound calm and positive* '—you'll have a captain of our air force to take over your training, as well as a naval diver to teach you combat swimming. It's important that you learn to—'

'Um, right.' Now both brows were up. 'Care to tell me why this is an important part of my training?'

'As king, you'll be head of the armed forces. Defence is vital to Hellenia—so it's crucial that you understand some of what they do.'

'So when does the army make its appearance?'

'You'll receive weekend-reserve training for three months before coronation.'

He groaned and shook his head. 'Why do I feel a Village People song coming on? When does the YMCA join in?'

Relieved he was taking it so well—she'd feared he'd get all caustic about the restrictions of everything he was expected to do—she laughed. 'So long as you don't invite Rasputin along, it will be fine.'

'That was Boney M, princess.' He chuckled when she made a rueful face. 'It was way before our time—and I don't suppose you attended many school dances.'

'Make that none. It's not in the required protocol, and created a security problem as well as the fear that I might—shock, horror—kiss an unsuitable local lad.' She sighed. 'I remember hating my entire family when the girls at boarding school put on their silky dresses, make-up and heels, and I was stuck in the dorm studying or reading.'

'Is the required protocol for everyone in the royal family, even extended members?'

'Only since someone took a potshot at my uncle when I was a child, and called us the offshoot of lowly soldiers.' She grinned wryly. 'Grandfather laid down new rules to protect us and keep us alive. I hated him for it for a long time. I didn't feel protected, I felt like—a freak.'

Strangely enough, Charlie didn't back off; his eyes were dark with empathy. 'I didn't grow up royal, but, especially in the past fifteen years, Papou separated us from things he felt were beneath us, especially Lia…' He started to say something else, frowned and closed his mouth—not shutting her out, but thinking.

*Well, he has a lot to think over,* she thought. *He hasn't even been here a day…he has to be on information-overload by this point.*

On *everything* overload, thanks to those fires he'd fought, the jet lag he was suffering, her blurting mouth and Grandfather's attacks.

'I'll leave you to sleep,' she said with a smile she hoped was encouraging, kind—all the things Grandfather hadn't been since Charlie's first words. And she was about to find out why. 'I'll make certain nobody bothers you until you come down for breakfast—lunch—whatever time it is.'

Charlie's face warmed as he smiled down at her. 'Thanks, princess. I'll be more human by then.' It wasn't a hopeful sentence, it was a vow. He was a man who knew himself, had mastery of his body…unless he was thrust into a new life without warning.

'Today's been enough to unsettle anyone.' She thrust out her hand.

'Thanks for understanding.' Ignoring the outstretched hand, he bent and kissed her cheek. It wasn't sexual, didn't linger, and yet she knew she'd feel it for hours…

'Good night.' She turned and walked down the hall with a slow, measured tread. She could show she was in control too.

And right now she needed control. She was about to rattle the cage of a king.

She stalked down the stairs and into the dining room, prepared for battle. 'What was that, Grandfather? Why are you attacking Charlie all the time? What's going on in your head, to push away our only and brightest hope for the future after a few hours?'

'I just wanted to make sure you're okay,' Charlie said awkwardly into the phone.

It was weird, to say the least. Though they were

in the same place, he had to call his own sister because they were so far apart. It reminded him of the time she'd been in the clinic, and he'd *hated* that. He never wanted to feel as lost and helpless again.

'I'm fine,' Lia said, on a yawn. 'A bit wired, that's all. I'm finding it hard to sleep. I think I'll see if they have a gym or a place I can dance off the jet lag.'

'You don't have your points,' he said, angry again. Why wouldn't they at least let them go home to pack?

His sister laughed. 'Check your cupboards, Charlie. They obviously have complete dossiers on us, what we like and how we work off stress. I have new points, a CD player and no less than four workout-suits.'

Charlie took the cordless phone over to the wall-length wardrobe. Besides the required suits, there was running gear and a choice of three of his favoured shoes, as well as a complete golf set—Taylor, no less.

It filled him with fury to have his privacy thus invaded—but obviously it didn't bother Lia. She didn't need to talk out her fears and emotions with him; she just wanted to dance. But when had she ever talked out her closest feelings with him? It was always Toby she turned to, and Toby wasn't here. What would happen when she did fall and Toby couldn't pick her up?

*It's not Lia falling at the moment, is it? It's you, and you're the one who seems to want help.*

He said goodnight, wished her happy dancing and hung up grimly, his heart hurting as he realized for the first time that, much as he loved his sister, she was as distant as starlight sometimes. She did keep her secrets.

It must run in the blood. No wonder she and Jazmine had become friends so fast.

*Jazmine.* Even her name got him all hot and bothered. Why couldn't she be Jane or Sally, a name that didn't roll off his tongue or his mind with a lush, silken sensuality reminiscent of seven veils? He'd have to keep calling her princess, or he might end up doing something he'd regret. For life.

Damn Papou for putting him in this position! Damn her, too, for showing him that Papou had by his training prepared Charlie to come here. Damn his own conscience for forcing him to keep to his word, for seeing the work to be done in this shattered place.

He had to stay the month out, or be tortured by his conscience the rest of his life.

He wouldn't sleep yet. He jerked on one of those immaculate tracksuits and new shoes, left his room, stalked back down the hall, down the stairs and out through the tea room to the balcony and gardens. He needed air, and space.

As soon as he was free of the beautiful sandstone walls and pink granite balconies, he broke into a run. It had only been two days since he'd discovered his heritage, and he'd already blown it more times than he could count. How many mistakes would he make in a month, let alone a lifetime?

*Oh, please, God, take me back three days in time so I can disappear…*

Exhausted from his run through the forest behind the gardens, embarrassed by having to ask the damn goons the way back, Charlie stalked down the hall, past his silent minders into his room, his thoughts still in a jumble, filled with worry, stress and—

No! He had to stop thinking about Jazmine. Even her name turned him on!

But it was hard to not think about her when inside the locked suite, with cameras and security everywhere, sat the object of his lust, smiling at him.

*My* forbidden *lust. Never forget that. Remember the price tag.*

But she was there on the exquisite ivory-and-gold *chaise longue*, her bare feet tucked beneath her. And, though she was in the formal attire the king had demanded they wear for dinner, she'd undone a few buttons, shrugged off the jacket and she'd let her hair down. *Where's a fire when you need to run?* Soft, tumbling loose curls of silky brown, framing her face like lush, dark silken veils... And that tiny, curving quarter-smile that said, 'I know you want me, but can you afford me?'

No, no, *no*. Not now and not ever.

Taking a chair opposite, he sprawled in inelegant abandon. 'So, wassup, princess?' he drawled with deliberate crudeness, flicking his fingers, watching them instead of her.

He didn't need to look. Her face was laser-burned into his memory, etched in his mind in every bright spot and hidden corner.

'Must be important for you to break protocol and risk the sensibilities of the goons outside,' he went on before she could speak. 'How'd you get around them?'

Her smile was as beautiful as sunlight on snow and as deadly as an ice pick, chipping away at his self-control smile by smile, hit by hit. 'There's a secret passage that runs from behind this room to the library.' The smile grew a touch. *Chink...touch her. Chink again, kiss her; just kiss her.* 'My brother Angelo and I found it when we were children. There're twelve passages going to a major passage leading to about a mile from here, in the forest. One leads from every royal suite. This house used to belong to the Orakis family, you see. They needed a series of escape routes for when their enemies attacked, or the people rose up in revolution…again.'

His brows lifted. Despite himself, he felt the intrigue growing. 'How many years did you spend looking for them?' he asked, to banish his interest in Hellenican history and all its attendant dangers. But the curiosity remained, and was growing hourly.

*You can help the people on a far more lasting scale…*

Her rogue dimple came and went; her eyes held that lurking twinkle. 'Who says I've stopped looking? Nothing beats the secret thrill of sneaking outside the palace walls at night with nobody the wiser.' She winked.

He grinned outright now. Man, this girl was charming, right at the moment when he wanted her to be…

No, he just *wanted*.

She was too dangerous by half, this Da Vinci darling. And didn't she know it, despite what Max thought? The look in her eyes said it all.

'So are you going to tell me why you're here, princess, or will we continue playing twenty-questions for a while?'

She was silent for a moment. 'If we are, I believe it's my turn. Why do you become so rude every time you feel threatened? Is it exhaustion, a defence mechanism you've used for a long time, or only against my family?'

Taken aback by her perspicacity, yet enjoying the game she'd begun, he said, 'Oh, your family is reason enough for rudeness, princess.'

Her brow lifted now. 'As an entity, or as royalty?'

He shrugged. 'Either will do, or both. Take your pick.'

'It won't work with us,' she said, her eyes soft-shimmering again. 'We're used to the stories made up by paparazzi, the encroaching attitude of the wannabe's, you name it. People of all walks of life feel they have the right to say what they like to us, or intrude on our privacy. We're used to it.'

'I'm not.' His enjoyment of the game they'd been playing faded abruptly. 'And it isn't something I *want* to become used to, princess.'

'Ah, you have your armour on again. You're calling me princess, locking me out. I understand. You've had a hard few days, and this must rank as the most overwhelming day anyone ever went through.' She rose to her feet and headed for the back wall. She looked at him over her shoulder, and the little, maddening smile told him she saw right through him.

Well, two could play at that game.

'You opened the door, princess,' he said lazily. 'I just didn't step through it at call. I've never been a "here, boy" kind of guy.'

The smile vanished. Her eyes grew wary, but she turned back around to face him. 'You have something to say.' She wasn't backing down.

He shrugged. 'I've said it already. I'm not into repeating myself. I like my life at home. I enjoy playing the field.' He looked her over. 'I'd ask you to dinner under different circumstances.'

'Which circumstances—my position, or the press?'

'Again, take your pick.' He continued making the words slow, lazy. As if he didn't care—because he didn't.

*Liar. You care, or you wouldn't be here. And Her Royal Pain in the Butt knows it as well as you do.*

'As I told you before, this isn't about me,' she said, with penetrating insight. 'For you, it's about going home and returning to your life. For me, it's about eight million lives that could become much better or worse, depending on your decision.'

Though his jaw clenched, hating the thought that he could hurt anyone by simply going home, he clapped once, twice. 'Good one, princess. That's the spirit. If you can't win me over with bribes, your looks and bedroom visits, by all means try the guilt trip. It's guaranteed to work on the average Greek boy.'

'Or Hellenican,' she smiled, though her cheeks tinged pink in acknowledgement of his shot. 'We are related to the ousted Greek royal family, though distantly.'

'It's working,' he said bluntly. In truth, he hadn't even been here a day and he felt the tug of duty clinking the iron collar gently around his neck. 'But there are some things I don't understand.'

He saw the tender fire leap into her eyes—at the thought of his agreeing to help her beloved people. He'd never met a woman so turned on by the notions of duty. 'What's that? Anything I can do to help…'

Though part of him didn't want to alienate her, he made himself say it. 'Can I still become king if I remain single? Do I lose it all if I refuse to marry you? In other words, is the whole shebang at the king's discretion?'

She'd stiffened before he finished speaking. Her face was white, her eyes holding shadows, but still she answered honestly. 'The position is yours to take, but the choice on marriage is yours to make—so long as she's of the right connections and power. In short, she must be someone the people and press will accept, and is in a position to help Hellenia. Grandfather will press you on the matter: I'm the best qualified to be your helpmate in making the best decisions for the nation. And the people will expect it.'

So, in other words, it was 'marry me or some other royal', but that was the limit of his choices, he thought grimly. And how many single princesses were there in Europe?

'What about Lia? What's the truth about her choices?' he asked, hating the look on her face—the same kind of mute suffering he'd seen on the Save the Children posters that had made him support three villages. She was no royal spoiled-brat in designer clothes and limos; she really *cared* about her people. 'If I refuse to take the position, can Lia choose to take it? Can she marry Max...or not? Is her position dependent on my decision, or her marriage to him?'

She was watching the slow-setting sun through his western-facing window. 'She doesn't *have* to marry Max, but he's the only man remotely suitable for the hand of a princess in Hellenia, besides you. As the law stands, she can't marry below the rank of Grand Duke—and, if she tries, there will be anarchy again. Our people have…expectations of us. *Strong* expectations. It's not Grandfather alone, though he has the ultimate power.'

'But the king likes her,' Charlie said slowly. 'Better than he likes me.'

Her hands balled into fists. 'Who wouldn't like her? Lia will make a magnificent princess. She was born for the role. I think Grandfather would still do his best to push her into a marriage with Max. There's nothing to dislike with him, is there?' She looked at him, with a deep keenness. 'Unless…is there a prior attachment? Is she in love?'

'No.' He frowned again as he thought of it. Lia was twenty-six, and she'd never fallen in love.

He shook himself, coming back to the present conversation. Despite doing his best to alienate Jazmine—and he believed he had—he couldn't restrain the admiration, looking at the upright figure, the quiet strength and dignity in every line of her. Even at the thought of losing the only thing she wanted, she still told the truth. He was sure the king would want her head for it, too.

Jazmine Marandis was a woman of integrity and courage.

'Thank you for your honesty.' What else was there to say? Reassurance was ridiculous at this point; he didn't know her well enough. He wasn't a man to her; he was a means to an end. She might find him as attractive as he found her, but that wasn't enough to base a lifetime of sacrifice on.

Not for him, anyway. It seemed she'd take him on, but the thought of her taking him as a noble sacrifice turned his stomach, no matter how attracted she was to him.

'You'd better go before your guys come looking,' he said.

At that, the glimmering smile returned. 'What, the big tough fireman's afraid I'll create a scandal to force a wedding?'

'I don't know about you, but, from what I've seen of the old guy, I have no doubt he'd do it,' he retorted, laughing despite himself.

The dimple peeped out as she grinned. 'I wouldn't put it past him at all.'

He said abruptly, 'He doesn't think I'm good enough to be prince.'

At the abrupt words, she leaned forward. 'He's set in his ways, Charlie. Just because he's a king doesn't make him less human—a crabby old man with gout and a heart reliant on a battery of pills, morning and night. He's used to clicking his fingers and having exactly what he wants.' She lifted her hands in an elegant kind of shrug. 'He doesn't want to understand that, without the training and all the years spent at Eton and Oxford, you couldn't be another Max.'

He felt the lines of his body relax. 'I understand that. Papou adored us, but it didn't stop him yelling at us on his bad days, or grunting at us on his good days.'

She chuckled softly. 'Just remember, Charlie, the decision is yours, not his. Old people don't like change, don't like being defied or criticized. He wants someone to carry on life as he did. Though he knows it won't happen, he doesn't have to be happy about it, just as his father was unhappy with him.' Her eyes shimmered with sweet mirth. 'Don't let him fool you; he was a rebel with a temper in his time.'

It took a few moments to digest the vision of the regal old boy in a leather jacket on a bike, upsetting the king before him. When he looked again, the princess was moving like shadows in the dusk to the back wall. 'Don't tell anyone about the passages.'

'It's our secret,' he returned as softly. She'd given him a gift tonight. He could at least try to return it.

He watched her as she ran her hand along the panelling in the wall, and a door appeared. She

turned to him for a moment, with a look com-
pounded of mischief, sadness, and something
almost like regret. Then she was gone, and only
the soft breeze from the passageway lingered: a
faint scent of pine-forest and loam. And then,
carried on the breeze, was a touch of roses, vanilla
and woman... And, just like this afternoon, the
thought and scent of her inspired tossing and
turning and very little sleep.

# CHAPTER SIX

*Ten days later*

FRESH back from an hour with Lia, seeing her delightful enthusiasm at trying each of her new duties, and her graceful dancer's ability to get so much right so quickly, Jazmine returned to her lessons with Charlie.

'I can manage a simple handwriting session alone, princess,' he'd drawled, and she'd sensed he needed time on his own.

But it was obvious it wasn't so simple for him. He was sitting on the high-backed chair with tight spine and straight shoulders, trying to turn his left-handed scrawl into the elegant, flowing script Grandfather demanded. He barely moved, apart from his arm and shoulder, but his hand looked awkward, curved over itself as he tried to write sitting like a statue. Though he said nothing, she sensed his discomfort and sense of failure.

He'd put up with the long list of 'must haves' with stoic silence and taut-jawed acceptance: 'Straight shoulders, Charlie... Your signature must be legible, with the Marandis elegance... You aren't rushing to a fire; you are His Royal Highness, Prince Kyriacou... Slow down the stride. Make it formal and deliberate, but with all your innate strength... Your tie must be straight when in public, meeting officials or at a press conference... Your chin should be half an inch higher—no, not an inch. It is that half-inch that separates regal pride from haughty indifference.'

As well as reading the Australian newspapers daily to keep up with home news, he read the classics and European news—in both Hellenican and Greek. He was also learning French, German and Italian: an hour's lesson for each language each day.

On Charlie, his silent stoicism was more frightening than his outbursts. His self-control sat on him like the suits he was forced to wear: *this isn't me.*

Hours of this every day would be enough to break anyone's spirit. Grandfather had decreed nine to ten hours a day, every day, for the month. *He has to know what he's in for, girl.*

Jazmine had always hated her lessons in royal behaviour and protocol, and she'd only endured four hours three times a week. She'd had years to get it right, not a few weeks—and she felt miserable and confused that *she* was holding the whip over his head.

Lia's intensive lessons were at a far easier pace, her 'royal list' far shorter.

Charlie seemed to be good at waiting, for a man with a temper. The paradox confused her. All her life—the people she'd known, the world she inhabited—had been about self-control...but not Charlie's kind. The self-control was real, living side by side with a volcanic temper and a brotherly love that never reproved but only gave.

She'd never known a man like him, had never seen family love as Lia and Charlie shared— and often lately she'd found herself wishing Grandfather had been the one to abdicate and run away to the other end of the planet.

As she watched him—she could barely take her eyes off him these days, so deep had her fascination become—Charlie's mouth turned right and grim as he tried again for an elegant signature. His knuckles were white.

'That's enough for now,' she heard herself say as she crossed the room to him.

He looked up at her, frowning. 'It's not even time for afternoon tea.'

She repressed the grin. He'd worked out Grandfather's habits, all right. Work only stopped at meal or tea times. 'Your hand's cramping,' she pointed out gently. 'And don't argue with me, please. I am the teacher, and I say enough. How about we take a walk in the gardens to relax, or spend some time in the gym?'

'Don't let me off the hook, princess.' His voice was tight now. 'It's not as if you have pure gold here. There's a lot of dirt to wash away, and not much time to do it.'

She shook her head. 'You don't have to be perfect, Charlie. As I told you, Grandfather wants you to be just like him, to carry on the life and traditions he began, and that won't work in the twenty-first century.'

'You think mine will work?' he asked dryly. 'The Crown Prince's pub diet: instigate beer after work, meat pie and chips Monday, fish and chips Friday?'

'A rough diamond?' she suggested with a smile. 'It might be a refreshing change for all of us.'

He shrugged, an eloquent movement that indicated his comfort with whom he was. 'Problem is, princess, I can pretend to be what I'm not; I might even convince some people I'm okay at it. But the man I am is obviously not acceptable.'

'To whom?' she retorted, feeling uncharacter-

istically heated. 'I told you, the king has no juris-
diction here. *You* are the heir, and the changes
we're working on are mainly cosmetic.' To her
inner shock, she realized how true it was. She
didn't *want* to change the man he was inside. She
liked him—more than liked him—just as he was.

'He's right, princess,' he said quietly. 'We both
know this is only the start. I have to know what
the world's doing and its relation to Hellenia,
how each country interacts with us, and what
problem we have with them. The cosmetic stuff
will only get me to the photo shoots. If I don't win
the respect of other rulers and diplomats—'

'Don't quote Grandfather to me!' she snapped.
'He had *years* to get this right, and even then he
rebelled. He has no right to treat you as he does—
and I don't know why he does it. I have never
heard him speak to a member of the royal family
with such—'

'Disrespect, bordering on contempt?' he put in,
when she broke off. 'Water off a duck's back,
princess. What I learn from him is more important than how he does it.'

She stared at him. 'He didn't offend you with
his attitude?' He'd certainly offended her.

Charlie shrugged. 'He might have, if I didn't
understand why he's doing it. It's for Hellenia,

and he's got to push me. It's good practice, anyway. If I take this on, I'm going to get plenty of disapproval and disrespect. If I let one opinion break me, how will I handle the press and the people?' He saw her frown at him, and grinned. 'Do you think I *need* to waste time worrying about the opinion of people I don't know or care about?'

The moment of fragile understanding and accord vanished; all of a sudden the gap between them broke wide apart, like an earthquake fissure. 'You'll *have* to care when they can sell the story and it will go worldwide. It will humiliate our people, and they've been through enough.'

The grin faded. 'That's the king's point, princess. So let's stop tap-dancing and tell it like it is.'

'Yes, let's.' She turned away, unable to stand it when his turbulent male beauty turned so self-mocking, wry with knowledge. It drew her like a lasso, dragging her to him. The only option was *not* to look. 'You've been learning for ten days what we've been learning from birth, and we still get it wrong. So, I repeat, he is too harsh on you— and you're way too hard on yourself. You're doing just fine.'

'If that's true, why aren't you looking at me when you say it?'

The blush crept up her cheek, but she turned to

him and said, 'I'm not used to teaching anyone, Charlie. I don't know how to say things—and when I look at you…'

'Yes?' He moved closer, until the fire inside him reached out and burned beneath her skin. 'When you look at me?'

His gaze mesmerized her, drew truth from her prim, proper training and scared little-girl's soul. 'When I look at you, I forget what I want to say.'

His eyes darkened; a finger touched her cheek. 'It's all new for you, isn't it, this wanting?' he whispered. 'Poor little princess wasn't given any armour for this fight.'

Her entire body quivered under the single touch; she melted beneath the untamed heat of him. He'd come to her—and, right now, despite his irreverent use of her title, he wasn't seeing her as a princess, but a woman. And having a man see her as something apart from her position was a rare event in her life. 'Yes,' she whispered. 'Um…I…I mean, no.'

His eyes darkened. 'If you keep looking at me like that, princess, you're going to get yourself thoroughly kissed by a rough commoner from Sydney.'

'You're not a commoner, and maybe I want to be kissed—*thoroughly kissed*—Charlie,' she whispered, couldn't bear to break the languid, sensual warmth floating between their bodies, their mouths, saying his name with the husky, blurry sound she knew made him hot for her.

His gaze dropped to her mouth with smouldering heat. 'For the first time, I'm sympathizing with arsonists,' he murmured, coming closer millimetre by delicious millimetre. 'I suspect a single kiss will turn into spontaneous and unstoppable combustion.'

'Charlie,' she breathed, her eyes fluttering shut as she leaned into him.

A gentle cough from the doorway of the private study that was their sanctum made them spring apart. 'Your Highnesses, the king requests your presence at your earliest convenience.'

'What is it?' Charlie snapped with obvious irritation at the interruption, and Jazmine wanted to smile.

The servant looked scared and backed out of the room without answering—and suddenly Jazmine thought she knew exactly why.

Without bothering to ask further, Charlie took her hand. 'Come on, princess.' He walked out of the room, but his stalking gait slowed when he noticed Jazmine rushing along in her high heels, half-afraid of stumbling. 'Sorry' was all he said, with the private smile that told her he hadn't forgotten the kiss they'd almost shared.

She almost pooled into a puddle of melted femininity at his feet.

Grandfather was lying on his recliner in the corner of his private reading-room, having a nap. He started to half-wakefulness when they entered. 'What is the meaning of this intrusion?' he barked, obviously to cover the embarrassment at being caught napping like any other elderly man.

'You tell us, sire,' Charlie said with cool respect, still holding her hand. 'We were told you wanted to see us immediately.'

Jazmine noted with sadness that, while Lia had progressed within days to calling the king Theo Angelis, and hugging him on greeting and good-night, Charlie remained on the most formal of terms with him.

A crafty look crossed her grandfather's face, and she knew she'd been right. The wily old fox. What was he up to? 'I see. I'm afraid I can't quite remember.'

At that, Jazmine lost it. 'Yes, you do. You gave specific orders for the servants to interrupt us if they saw us getting too close.'

Charlie turned to her, his face startled. Then, to her shock, he grinned and slowly started laughing—and kept laughing until he released her hand, doubling over.

*That* got Grandfather's full attention. He sat up straight, and asked in his frostiest tone, 'What is so funny about that, Kyriacou?'

Charlie kept chuckling. 'You only make me cross the world to marry her, and then you want to stop us kissing? I'm obviously missing something here.'

Grandfather frowned, but before he could speak Jazmine spoke. 'You broke your promise, Grandfather. You told me you wouldn't interfere for the month.'

His brows rose. 'Have I interfered with his royal training in any way?'

'Apart from the mile-long list of do's and don'ts, and setting servants to watch us?' she retorted, exasperated. 'I'm not sure. You tell me!'

Grandfather put on his haughtiest look. 'You are a princess of the blood, Jazmine. You will not behave in a common manner.'

'So she can't get it on with a commoner?' Charlie interrupted in a tone of mild query—deliberately drawing Grandfather's fire, she suspected. 'I thought that was the whole point of my coming here—to create satisfactorily royal offspring. The theory being that, though I was raised as a commoner, if I bleed it'll come out blue. But, hey, what do I know? I'm just a fireman with the necessary ancestry, right?'

Charlie grinned at her, and Jazmine felt her lips twitching; she felt furious and hilarious and touched. Nobody besides Max had stuck up for her for the longest time. But Charlie knew, had seemed to know from the first day, how to make her laugh. He could poke fun both at himself and at tradition and belief that, through a stranger's eyes, didn't seem so sacred—or so scary to change. And, oh, how she wanted to kiss him right now. Deep, long and hot. She wanted the kiss she'd been denied only minutes ago, to touch his skin like a lover, to trust him to show her the way. She'd been a porcelain piece kept on the shelf too long: 'look but don't touch; admire me from afar, because you can't afford me'.

But she'd come alive with one look at her turbulent prince; the princess had become a woman, and she didn't want to return to her starved, duty-only existence.

'You will withdraw the surveillance, Grandfather, and allow Charlie and me to bond in our time and way. You will also stop treating Charlie like the enemy. It's as if you're trying to force him to leave. He is *not* his grandfather, and *I* am his teacher, not you. I'm asking you to keep your promise to stay out of our personal business.'

A tiny shock ran through her as the look on her grandfather's face changed, and became tinged with something almost like respect overlaid with embarrassment. Jazmine flicked a glance at Charlie; it told her all she didn't want to know.

Charlie knew, or had at least suspected the source of the rudeness.

Grandfather *had* set him up to fail—and Charlie continued to meet each challenge with ice-cold control and stoic silence. He'd refused to let the old man beat him.

The fury she'd felt in the ballroom was now double-pronged. Was everything between these two a game?

Her mouth tightened. She waved an irritable hand, and turned on her heel. 'Do as you will; you both appear to be enjoying your games. You have my apologies for my interruption into your little "who's going to break first?" contest!'

The measured tread she used could in no way have been called storming out. If they wanted to win so badly, so be it. All she knew was that neither of them would be allowed to beat her down. And they could both grow up!

\* \* \*

Charlie gave her half an hour before he went looking.

He finally ran her to ground in the gym. She was on the walking machine, but she wasn't walking.

'You'll break it, at the rate you're pounding on this thing. You must be doing fourteen kilometres an hour,' he said, but she didn't answer.

He saw the MP3 player at her waist, the earpieces in her ears, and, with a grin, walked around so she'd see him.

She started and made a mis-step—and, at the speed she was running, it could have been lethal. He leaped toward her, arms extended so her torso would land into his arms, hips and waist; but before he touched her she'd grabbed the handrails, and after a couple of stumbles she was on track again. And she kept running as if he didn't exist.

She still hadn't got all her anger out. His grin grew. She must be really mad.

He turned and walked into the male dressing-rooms. He changed into designer running trousers and a tank top, and found his trusty old trainers, refusing the top brand waiting for him.

Within minutes he was walking beside her,

building up to a run. He'd prefer to be pounding the pavement, but the security issue would create a nightmare for the Secret Service, so he had to settle for what the secure gym could offer.

Jazmine kept running, looking straight ahead. The only things she seemed to notice were her water bottle and towel.

He'd never seen a more sensual sight than that water going down her throat, or seeing the towel grow damp from the perspiration she wiped from her forehead, throat, and chest. He was even turned on by her bouncing ponytail, the way some curls escaped from the band and grew wet against her nape and throat.

Man; he really had it bad.

How he could, he had no idea. Everything between them was prim, proper and correct. And, yet, he kept seeing her in his room, lying on the *chaise*, like the naughtiest invitation he'd never accepted…and wished he had.

So many layers to her; so many super-impositions, every one real and true. She wasn't acting with any of them, except perhaps 'the proper princess'. And every layer fascinated him—perhaps because the complexity made her less royal, more human.

No matter which layer she showed at the time, he wanted her more.

He wasn't stupid. He couldn't have her. She was too high, too clean, too *pure* for him. Despite the heated looks she gave him, he knew she was innocent: she didn't know she was looking at him like that. The sweet surprise in her eyes told him he was the first man to awaken her to the fact that she was a woman. She didn't want to make love; not yet. She wanted to feel pretty and feminine, to have flowers and go dancing, and all the things a normal girl had. But Jazmine wasn't normal, never had been and never would be—at least, not his version of normality.

Again he saw the parallels to Lia, to her life. No wonder they'd taken so well to each other. They were sisters under the skin, girls raised in opposite ivory-towers. Papou had protected Lia as well as King Angelis had protected Jazmine.

But now, Jazmine was cool and distant. Even after she'd made him reach flashpoint by caring about him, she'd done that incomprehensible woman thing and had turned into the ice maiden for no good reason he could see.

He'd put a crack in her composure again.

If he had to change his entire life to get this prince gig right, she could drop a few of her little mysteries, let go a little. If she wanted him for her future king, she could be more than that intriguing and lovely Mona Lisa. She'd be that stuttering, blushing, real woman she'd been when she'd admitted she wanted him.

The challenge was on: the royal and the ordinary Joe. Let the best player win.

So he kept running, using the water bottle and towel as she had, but letting the sweat rest on his skin a little longer than he ought to.

She never turned her head once.

After a twenty-minute run, he saw she was out of water. He took the bottle and refilled it for her while he refilled his.

She kept running; didn't even nod in thanks or acknowledgement. Charlie's grin grew. Missing her manners, was she?

He strolled over to the weights area, lay on the mat and began his crunches: a hundred of each, including cross-waist. He did them far more slowly than he would normally do. Why not? It was better for his body, and until she remembered the lessons he had a little free time. And he wasn't in her direct line of sight. Behind the chest-wall hydraulic machine, she'd have to crane her head to see him.

And she would—oh, she would. He'd knock

the invisible tiara right off her head with a little street smartness...

He didn't bother with the 'show off in the gym' stuff so many guys did—the kind of women he liked rarely fell for the obvious. They usually gave those guys a contemptuous smile and avoided them. When he finished his sit-ups, he moved to the corner of the room, out of her range of sight, where she'd have to actually turn her head to see him—she'd have to *want* to look.

And he began his favourite workout: chin-ups over the high bar.

It wasn't a show-off measure, either. A lot of his job entailed lifting himself into inaccessible places. He had to keep his fitness levels up. Could he help it if it showcased the muscles of his arms, shoulders and chest with every movement?

When he was done, he turned his head to look for her—and she was right behind him. Was the flush from the exercise, fury...or was she just a little excited?

'Princess,' he greeted her gravely.

'I have a name, firefighter,' she countered, with mirror-like composure, her eyes challenging.

His heart was still hammering, and from more than the exercise. 'Jazmine.'

Slow and deliberate, she ran her gaze over his

body, flushed and sheened with sweat. 'Have you finished your silent "how to" lesson in gaining muscle without bulk?'

Caught out—and willing, *glad*, to admit it—he nodded. Her lovely, curvy body was luminescent, shimmering. He wanted to rub himself over her skin like that towel...

The game was on. Both aroused, willing to show it—wanting so much more than just to look.

'Good,' she said softly. 'So tell me why Grandfather's riding you, and why you're letting him do it.'

The look in her big, angelic whisky-eyes was irrefutable. This adorable, hot and sweaty, kiss-me woman was setting boundaries at the moment his body began to scream. She'd pinned him to the mat when he'd least expected it—but her demand was honest. Even now she didn't know how to turn games to her advantage, and he liked that. Wanting a woman was natural to him; liking her was a bonus. *Respecting* her as deeply as he did Jazmine turned desire imperative.

Telling her wouldn't take the edge off—might even lend some piquant spice to the contest—and the victory.

'He doesn't hate my grandfather for his disappearance alone. He was angry about that, but hated him for who he took with him.'

Her eyes grew; her lush mouth fell open. 'Oh. So the woman he loved and lost was your grandmother?'

*Touch her, touch her, touch her...* He pulled himself together, tearing his gaze from her ready lips. 'He adored her, but she loved my grandfather. I look like Papou, have his name and his temper. Lia has Yiayia's name and her personality—her gentle ways, her way of defusing tension, and her smile.'

'It makes sense.' She nodded, looking so sweet and delightful with that little crinkling frown he ached, hard all over with the need to kiss her. 'And you don't mind that he so obviously favours Lia?' She peeped at him through her lashes.

Gone, gone; he was *so* gone. Unable to stop the surging king-tide taking over his body, he leaned forward, his mouth hovering near hers. 'It's not the old guy's favour I want,' he whispered against her mouth. 'I want you, Jazmine, I want you.'

A tiny moan escaped her throat, sexy and husky and *needing*. 'Char-r-r-lie...'

Absolutely and totally gone. He pulled her against him, loving the hot, slippery feel of her. The sweat made her human, a woman who wanted him and didn't know any games to put him off or make him wait. Her desire was clear to read in every look of those wide, new-woman's eyes, in the way she swayed into him, the aching yearning in the way she said his name.

But, as he was about to kiss her, she put a hand on his chest. 'The cameras. Tonight, Charlie… tonight. The secret passage,' she whispered.

Liking, lust, respect and a touch of the forbidden; how could he resist? He moved just a touch, so his mouth brushed hers with every movement. 'Tonight.'

# CHAPTER SEVEN

SHE was floating around the room. One moment she was sweetly smiling on that *chaise*, wearing something filmy and soft, her hair a silky cloud around her face and throat, the next she was coming to him through the closed balcony window, wearing only the most feminine of perfume. Driving him crazy, trying to catch her. Always beckoning to him with that tiny princess-wave he'd seen in photos: try to get close, I dare you...

Though he wanted to be strong, to resist her game, she'd whisper, 'Char-r-rlie,' with that incredibly arousing accent, and all his good resolutions crumbled to show the raw, elemental man beneath. Night and day, no matter what he was doing, she was there, in his mind if not in person. Making him ache for her simply by breathing.

'Jazmine,' he growled, and reached for her, but his arms found only cold air. He shivered, and in that instant she had vanished again, back to the land of impossible dreams and fairy tales. And he had what he wanted—he was just a normal guy, back in Sydney and in uniform, fighting a fire.

But the fire was in him. Toby was dousing Charlie in water and chemicals, but nothing put it out. He needed *her*—only she could make him stop burning and live…

He sat up abruptly in bed, amazed to find he wasn't soaked in sweat from the heat of the dream. The rose-and-vanilla scent of her filled his head; the ghost-lights from the garden and the silver half-moon flooded the night with unearthly radiance, illuminating the trailing clouds and the slender statue of a goddess on the edge of his balcony.

It looked like Jazmine, with that maddening half-smile she threw at him as she glanced over her shoulder. No wonder he couldn't stop dreaming about her.

Knowing he wouldn't sleep again for at least an hour, he got to his feet and threw open the balcony door, taking deep breaths of the sweet, fragrant summer air.

As if on cue, he saw a small, upright figure wandering amid the rose garden below his room, not wearing the shimmering, filmy thing from his dream, but, in a simple blue summer-dress and peasant sandals, her hair unbound, she'd walked right into it.

So he wasn't the only one losing sleep. Why hadn't she come to him as she'd promised?

As if sensing him, she turned. Her eyes met his, limpid shadows in the deeper dark, her hair touched with gilt by the lights above. She took a step towards him.

It was a tiny movement. Then Charlie saw the minders behind, and remembered the one always out on his balcony, watching. He waved, as if that was all either of them had intended, when they both knew.

Her chin lifted—a small, haughty nod for the sake of their unwanted audience—then she allowed her face to come into the light. Her eyes asked the question.

Heart pounding in anticipation, he nodded. He watched as she turned to the path leading back to the palace, then he returned to his room and closed the doors.

Waiting.

He sat in the warm, silvered dark for almost fifteen minutes before the quiet clicking sound came, and she slid in from the secret passage. Her eyes were shining. 'Come with me,' she whispered. Her hand made the little gesture that always seemed to say—to him at least—'come and get me'.

Unable to deny that he'd go wherever she beckoned, he followed her.

Within moments they were plunged together into soft, welcoming darkness. Every sense was heightened; he was aware of everything he couldn't see. A warm hand slipped into his. He felt her rise up on her toes, angling towards him. Warm breath touched his ear. 'There are light- and movement-sensors above the ceiling—not close, but not that far. We can't make any sudden movement, or any noise above a mouse.'

He shuddered with the rush of hot desire. Her touch, her whispered words, roared to life in him. His fingers closed around hers with a caressing motion. He moved his face until cheek touched cheek, and he nodded. 'Let's go,' he whispered, and felt her shiver.

He didn't ask where, and she didn't ask if he wanted to know. She led and he followed, and they both knew: what was here.

What was coming.

There was a peculiar intimacy in the tunnel. Holding hands, they moved foot by foot, free hands touching the wall. It was like connection, as if the tunnel was a friend, as if they were friends.

Were they? He didn't know, didn't know if
being with her now was a good thing or a disas-
trous thing. All he knew was she'd shimmered
into his soul with the sheerness of a gossamer
dream, seducing him with her courage and
strength, her honesty and sweetness and big-eyed
prettiness…and he trusted her.

She should be the enemy. God knew she repre-
sented everything he wanted to run from. But it
was as if he stood in sinking mud and couldn't
move from her. Because of her, he couldn't run,
couldn't hide, he could only be himself—do his
best to jump all the hurdles set for him, and hope
what he offered was good enough.

Good enough for the Hellenican people, and
good enough for her. He'd run from responsibility
for others all his life, even from Lia's illness. It
was always Toby who'd done the hard work—the
emotional stuff—with his sister.

He wasn't going anywhere, not yet. He
wouldn't shirk his responsibility. He couldn't—
no, he wouldn't—leave Jazmine in the lurch.

*Jazmine.* The name was a drumbeat in his blood.

He bumped into her when she turned to the left.
About to mouth an apology, he felt her turn and
touch her finger to his lips.

A finger. Such a little thing to send a furnace

rip-roaring through him. It was too late now, too late for talk, too late to wait. Jazmine, Jazmine; *I have to have her; I have to have her; I've got to.*

Using his free hand, he touched her waist, asking, not commanding. Not because she was a princess, because she was a woman with too few choices in her life. He let it rest for a moment while he waited for her answer, and his blood thudded in his ears and pounded in his head and he hoped.

Her soft intake of breath, a gentle move closer, was all the answer he needed. He bent—such a small woman to hold all that courage and self-sacrifice—and kissed her.

He missed. He could hear the sensuality in her quiet laugh as she wound her hands into his hair—she missed first time, too—and brought him in the right direction.

Almost.

Laughing without sound, bumping noses, their bodies moving to crowd into each other, they both whispered at the same time, 'Let's go outside.'

She took his hand again, and the rightness of it flooded his entire being. He didn't question it. He'd second-guessed too much lately. He wanted her, was with her, was touching her... and it was enough.

Something about that thought haunted him, something he ought to connect.

'The exit's just ahead,' she murmured as the passage began sloping up, and they stepped out into a wider cavern with filtered moonlight illuminating small patches. There were niches in the walls, the sites of old religious rituals. He stepped into an indent in the floor, and almost tripped over the rocks filling it. It looked, felt, smelled, incredibly ancient. He could see Greeks and Hellenicans of olden times living, working here, hiding their beliefs from those threatened by it.

Hellenicans sneaking into and out of a palace for lovers' trysts, for political meetings or sacred rites—running for their lives. This cave was silent witness to the rise and fall of kings, including his ancestors, and he could be the next to rise.

Somehow it felt right to be here with Jazmine.

He inhaled the scent of loam before Jazmine pushed aside a mess of bracken and vines covering the exit cave, and he knew where they were. Still clasping her hand, he looked around at the cool, dark forest surrounding them. 'Somehow I knew you weren't taking me into your bedroom.'

She laughed, low and sweet. 'The lack of stairs was probably your first clue.' Her face lifted to his, eyes glowing, lips curved in that secret woman-smile that made a man's heart yank from his chest and want to do a primitive victory-dance with it. 'No one can see us now,' she whispered, and added, 'And we can see each other.'

'It helps.' He smiled and drew her close, going slow, wanting to drag her to him and devour her, but the moment felt too important to rush it.

He didn't know what he'd expected when they kissed—fireworks, fire, or at least an explosion of passion. What he hadn't expected was this, a soft, dreaming adagio of innocence. A slightly clumsy, laughing, joining of their souls.

The missing kisses in the passage, the bumping of noses, had been a prelude to the real thing. A shivering rapture, yet tender as a moth's wings touching him. Her skin was silk, her mouth honey, her smile, even as they kissed, magic.

The bungee-jumping in the dark that had been his life since he'd found out he was the 'grand what of where?' felt worth it when he touched Jazmine. Everything that scared him most came with touching this woman—and, yet, she was everything he'd ever wanted. He wanted to bolt, yet at the same time he wanted to live for her, and her alone.

Just as the laughter and rippling sweetness of a hidden waterfall refreshed the heart and soul, so did holding Jazmine in his arms, kissing her smiling mouth, feeling her cool, gentle fingers exploring his skin. So innocent, yet it was *him* trembling like a virgin. He felt like he had when he'd kissed his first girl on her front doorstep: like he was jumping the moon, and expecting a shotgun to his head when her dad busted them.

The shotgun was already there with Jazmine; he hadn't forgotten the price that came with having her. But he couldn't make himself care, not now, not when with a simple moving of mouth on mouth it felt as if he held the beauty of misted moonlight in his arms, the untouchable magic of laced fairy-ice in the forest above him.

He almost laughed aloud. How ironic that, after all these practical years, he'd turned into some sixteenth-century poet. How Toby would laugh at him, and call it 'poetic justice'! But it was what he felt, and he couldn't stop kissing her. He couldn't.

'We need to talk, Charlie,' she said softly against his mouth minutes, hours, later. He didn't know.

'Yeah.' He kissed her again. 'Soon…'

Having her against him, fluid and feminine, and *Jazmine*, made him feel…

It was stupid, ridiculous, but there was no other word for it: *complete*. Like two jigsaw pieces he'd spent a lifetime trying to find a fit; like jagged shards of porcelain that came together to make something exquisite. That was Jazmine in his arms.

Questioning 'why' would destroy it, so he didn't. He held her and kissed her and ignored the moments becoming minutes.

'Charlie…'

'Jazmine…' He touched his forehead to hers, aching to kiss her again, but knew her determination. 'If we have to talk, *loulouthaki*, then talk.'

He had no idea why he'd called her 'little flower', but, again, it fit. Perhaps it was her name, which meant 'star flower'; perhaps it was because, like little flowers that grew in inaccessible hills and rocks, she clung: to life, to hope, to doing what was right.

A smile flitted across her face at the nickname. Then slowly, as if she ached too, she nodded and pulled away from him to a rock near the cave entrance, and sat looking at her hands. Perhaps that was because she dared not look up into his tense face, his aroused male body. 'I couldn't come earlier. Grandfather…'

'I thought so,' he said quietly. 'Crazy, isn't it? He wants us to marry, but doesn't want it to be anything but a business arrangement.'

'It's what he had with my grandmother,' she sighed.

Charlie frowned. 'So?'

'So it's all he understands, Charlie. "Duty is its own reward" is his motto.'

'He loved Yiayia.'

'And never had her to lose. He had women. We all knew about his women. But none were her, you see, so they were just…' She shrugged. 'It's said the Marandis men only love once, and for ever. That he was stuck with the duty while your grandfather had the happiness? It's no wonder he turned duty into a sacred privilege.'

'And no wonder he takes it out on me. I came here mocking all he holds dear, all he knows.' He came to her. Something in her body said 'don't touch me', so he sat beside her on the rock. The size of it precluded personal space, which was fine with him, but she moved. An inch had never seemed so wide as now, when she wouldn't bridge it. 'I can handle it, Jazmine. Because he's determined to beat me, the old guy's got more energy than I think he has had in a long time.' He grinned. 'I wouldn't mind betting he and Papou were friends and competitors at one time.'

She sighed and nodded. 'You're right—he has been enjoying it. It isn't that.' She sounded odd; haunted. 'But he had chest pain again tonight. His lips turned blue.'

Knowing how quickly Papou had gone downhill with his heart, he didn't need a lesson in colour-by-numbers. 'How long do you think we have before the press gets wind of his illness, and the fact that I'm here?'

She shifted another inch, until she was almost falling off the rock. 'A few days. Somebody's bound to tell, no matter how many confidentiality contracts we have signed. Charlie…' She closed her eyes and spoke in a tone reminiscent of the pain in ripping off a plaster. 'I need to know what you're feeling about it.'

Again, he didn't pretend to misunderstand. He frowned and looked away, to the ghostly shapes of the trees outlined by the slow-dipping moon, wishing they were still kissing. This use of their mouths seemed a damned pointless exercise. 'Hell if I know, princess.'

She rose to her feet and walked over to the curtain of bracken and thorns. She fingered them as if blinded and finding her way by touch. 'We have to be ready.'

'How am I supposed to know, Jazmine? I'm locked in a room with you. And, while you're telling me how to walk, talk, sit, stand, write, and how to wear suits that would cost me a month's wages back home, I'm thinking about making love to you.'

Her breath hitched so fast she hiccupped. 'I—' *Hiccup*. 'Char—' *Hiccup*.

He smiled, satisfied she was still thinking about it as much as he was. 'But while all that's important, what has it got to do with the real job? What good does looking and sounding like Australia's answer to Prince Charming do me in making a decision that changes more lives than just mine?'

Her fingers stilled over a thorn; she obviously dug in too deep, and she made an impatient noise and popped her finger into her mouth. And he wished he was that finger, warm and cocooned by her lips.

'Again, you're right,' she said quietly. 'You need to know what you're facing—politically, socially and intellectually—to—to see.'

'To see if I can fill your grandfather's shoes, or if I'll end up letting the country and family down, and taking off like my grandfather,' he filled in grimly. 'That's what worries the old guy most, isn't it—that I'm so much like Papou?'

She sighed and nodded.

He hadn't noticed that he'd made fists of his hands until he scraped them against the rock. 'It seems to me the Danes had it right when they got their Australian import: they took her to the palace and gave her a few years to see if she could handle the life.'

'They're lucky enough to be a constitutional monarchy,' Jazmine said quietly. 'Hellenia isn't yet—and Denmark doesn't have a man like Orakis waiting in the wings to take over, should you—I mean we—'

She bit her lip.

'I think the word you're looking for is "fail".'

She turned to him, her eyes limpid in the darkness, lovely—and worried. 'That's not what I believe, Charlie.'

'That makes one of us, at least.' He couldn't help the harshness in his voice—and she had to know it wasn't aimed at her.

At that, she came back to where he sat, sat beside him, and took his hand in hers. 'There are worse things than making mistakes, such as never trying.'

He turned to look at her, at that pretty face so mysterious and so giving at once. 'You're the one who said eight million lives depend on my getting it right.'

'No, I didn't. I said those lives depend on your *decision*.'

'Same thing, isn't it?'

'No.' She squeezed the hand she held. 'It's completely different. Whatever you decide affects my people. Your mistakes will affect them, too, but they'd forgive you, Charlie. Don't you see?' Her voice turned husky with passionate conviction. 'You'll make mistakes, I will too.'

He gave a short, derisive laugh. 'I don't believe that any more than you do. You know exactly what to do at any given moment, and everyone loves you for it.'

She stilled again, as if he'd really said something she didn't know. Then her hands curled over, the free hand into a fist, the other squeezing his fingers. 'If that was true, I'd know what to say to you to make you see what I see in you,' she mumbled.

He felt the burning urge to ask her what she meant, but it wasn't time for personal declarations, not when he didn't have a clue how *he* felt. This, tonight, was too momentous. He settled for saying, 'You're eloquent enough when you want to be.'

She sighed and fiddled with his fingers, sending a rush of scalding desire through his veins—and she wasn't even thinking about it. 'As I said, we'll both make mistakes—but they won't be mistakes that will see villages burned and people homeless. You'll never make mistakes from lack of caring.'

The words tapped into a core of something deep inside him. He didn't know exactly what, but, while what she'd said felt incredibly reassuring, it held the sense of putting his hand into a snake hole. Trusting her belief in him was beautiful and deadly—deadly dangerous to those who'd depend on him to get it right.

'Until I see the country for myself, and know what's going on and what's needed, I'll keep feeling like I'm walking blind in a minefield,' he said curtly, hiding the welter of confused, struggling emotions.

She nodded. 'Let's suspend lessons for now. We have decisions to make—me as well as you.'

He grinned. 'And it's hard to do that with the goon squad and Candid Camera watching our every move.'

She smiled and relaxed visibly. 'I'm due to meet with Lord Vedali, the Spanish ambassador, tomorrow, to discuss some vital matters of trade. Grandfather has been handing these meetings to me for the past year or more. I'd like you to come with me. In fact, I think you should take the meeting. He's a man of integrity as well as good sense, so we can rely on his discretion.'

Touched by her obvious faith, he smiled at her. 'I'll do my best.'

She glowed as if he'd handed her a diamond. Maybe he had. 'Thank you. It's tomorrow morning at ten.'

He checked his watch and grinned. 'I think you mean today, princess.'

'And didn't you enjoy telling me I'd gotten something wrong?' she retorted with a return smile. 'See, I'm not perfect.'

He laughed. 'Just ninety-nine percent?'

Instead of laughing at his joke, she frowned. 'Perfection is a real issue with you. If you don't do everything right first time, you think you're not good enough.'

A vision of Lia, collapsed on the ground, fainting from lack of food—and he hadn't even noticed until then—walked side by side with another: a young wife and mother dead, because he hadn't been there on time or done enough to save her.

And the biggest one of all…

*No, damn it, I won't go there again!*

He couldn't allow himself to even think about it. That way led to destruction, and he had Lia to care for. And, possibly, a whole damned country to run because the other candidate was a madman in a designer suit.

The fragile accord he'd been feeling with her, the gossamer beauty of their kiss, splintered and shattered as if it had never been. He stood up and yawned. 'It's time for sleep, if I'm going to take this meeting. I can barely think.'

'Yes,' she agreed. Her voice was quiet—too quiet.

He led the way in. When she tried to protest, he whispered coolly, 'If I take on the job, Your Highness, I just might need to know how to get out quick one day. It seems to be the way of this people.'

Very softly, she answered, 'If you won't believe in yourself and your ability to rule Hellenia, Charlie, then I'll have to believe for both of us.'

And he had no answer for her. He told himself he didn't want one.

As the silence dragged, she pulled him to a stop and went up on tiptoes. His heart knocked against his ribs, but she merely murmured in his ear, 'You don't know our ways, but you care—you want to do what's right. I believe that will carry you through the times you get things wrong—and the times I'll get it wrong as well. Even if I'm ninety-nine percent perfect, Charlie, that means I will still make mistakes some of the time.'

The way she said his name, a soft purr in his ear, heated his blood to boiling point—but he wasn't going down that path again. Not tonight.

He led the way back to his room in silence.

# CHAPTER EIGHT

WHY, *why*, had he eaten so much breakfast?

Stomach churning as he walked beside Jazmine through the ruined village, Charlie felt sick. He couldn't think of her as a princess, not with the sick baby in her arms and the tears in her eyes as she greeted people with so much caring.

Though Helmanus had a similar beautiful forest-setting to others they'd passed this morning, with rolling verdant hills and trees abounding, and there was the scent of sage and lemongrass and soft loam everywhere, not one house was whole. Each house had a part that had been burned or blasted away. The street had dark patches on the stones that cried out their memories of suffering. The graveyard had more fresh headstones than the village had people.

Widows and orphans were everywhere, and elderly folk who had made shrines to sons and daughters who'd died trying to preserve their way of life…or had died just because they'd been there.

He couldn't believe he'd ever thought he'd be worse than Orakis as a guardian over the Hellenican people. He'd been so focused on going home, and so appalled about the intrusions of the press, and feeling trapped by living in a palace with minders, when these people had so little…
*Nothing.*
No, they had Jazmine. Right now, nobody could throw the 'Mona Lisa' taunt at her. She held the baby with such tenderness, not seeming to care that his wet nappy and less-than-pristine baby clothes were soiling her designer suit. She spoke to the people about their needs, about what had been done and what was coming next, with thorough knowledge and complete empathy. She ignored the flashing of the cameras, refusing to answer questions on her clothing or love life, but answering the questions on conditions here with passion, conviction and vision. Her eyes still kept her secrets, but, standing close in his minder's role, Charlie could see the stress beneath, the burdens she'd chosen to take upon herself.

A tug at his trouser leg made Charlie look down. A child stood there, her hair neatly plaited and her dress a touch too tight for her. Her sandals were broken.

She smiled as she held out her hand to him.

The confidence in her eyes shook Charlie to the core. The child expected him to give to her because he was with Jazmine. Jazmine, who was quietly pressing money into people's hands with no fanfare. Jazmine, who'd arranged for the cars in their retinue to be filled with food. The security men were handing out flour, oil, fruit and vegetables, care packs hidden in hemp sacks.

'Do it,' Jazmine whispered through lips barely moving, moving the baby up to her shoulder to cover her words to him. 'Behave as the others do, or the press will wonder why you're different.'

At that moment, Charlie knew why she'd insisted he wear the anonymous dark suit and sunglasses of the Secret Service. In this disguise, he was invisible to the press.

Though she needed his cooperation to ensure the ongoing wellbeing of these desperate people, or even to become queen, Jazmine protected his privacy. She respected his right to choose his future.

Was there no one whose welfare this woman didn't place before her own?

He handed out coins and sacks of food. As he looked around to find more in need, trucks began arriving. When the drivers unloaded, the people cried aloud in joy.

Building materials. Tiles for roofing. Bricks to

fill holes in walls. Glass panes and shutters to replace those in splinters. Mats for floors.

And bags and bags of warm clothing and shoes against the forthcoming winter.

Some of it was second-hand clothing, it was obvious by the worn look of it, and the uneven heels of the shoes. But, new or old, to the people of Helmanus it was a gift direct from God.

And Jazmine was their guardian angel, no matter whose money was being spent.

As he handed Jazmine back into the car, the press took shots of him.

He knew that, if they reached Australian shores, his anonymity would soon end. Even in the dark suit and sunglasses, somebody would be bound to make the connection.

It was time to make the decision—and, damn it, after today it shouldn't be so hard. Didn't he *want* to help these people? Of course he did.

*But I want it to be as it's always been. I want to help in the disguise of a uniform, take my orders and then disappear with my friends to the pub. I don't want to have to wear a crown to help.*

He hated the selfishness that still lived in him even after facing the magnificent self-sacrifice that was Jazmine. But he couldn't deny that, while the woman was all he'd ever dreamed of, the princess in the public eye was his worst nightmare, and the deep-hidden core of truth he didn't want to look at, because it hurt too much. Because it would always be there, every day of his life, haunting him like the words he'd said at seventeen that had changed his world for ever.

*I don't want to make a stuff-up that could make things so much worse for these people. I couldn't stand to kill anyone else.*

'That photo will blow my privacy,' he said as they took off, and she was resting back against the leather with a sigh he couldn't interpret.

She didn't deny it. 'Given your recent fame, it probably will. If the Australian press connects you to the fireman hero, they'll start digging—and the Consulate's "no comment" will only make things worse. Prepare yourself. The story will probably leak within the next couple of days.'

He digested it for a few moments. 'You knew this would happen.'

Her eyes were still heavy from the tears she'd tried all morning to hide, combined with the tiredness of being in the forest with him last night. 'I thought it might.'

'Forcing the decision, princess?' he asked, with milder sarcasm than he'd have shown two weeks ago.

She didn't even look at him. 'You didn't have to be the one to help me into the car. You could have chosen to fade into the background.' A tired hand passed over her eyes. 'Ask yourself who is forcing the pace here, Charlie. Ask yourself who is the one who's changing.'

He didn't want to think about it, didn't want to see the truth in her assertion; but he couldn't help looking at her. She was pale, her lashes fluttering over closed eyes. 'Come here.' He wrapped an arm around her shoulder, and pulled her close enough to remove the pins from her hair, the silk scarf from her throat. 'Better?' he asked quietly.

With a weary sigh, her head rested against his shoulder. 'Much.'

The mumble was so tired. They'd left for the village before seven, and it was after two now. She'd eaten with the villagers at their invitation, but she hadn't eaten much, refusing to take food from their mouths.

It didn't hurt to help her out after all she'd been through today. He moved slowly back until they were against the leather. 'You did good today, princess.'

'So did you. I knew you would.' She sighed, halfway to sleep. 'And the money is better spent here than lying useless in a Swiss bank account.'

He blinked and made the connection in an instant. 'Whose money did you spend today, Jazmine?'

A tiny smile. 'I like it when you say my name: *Zhahz-meen*. You make it sound so lovely. I feel pretty when you say it.'

Despite his recent fears, he couldn't help but grin at the sleepy confession. The woman hiding beneath the picture-perfect princess peeked outside whenever they were alone—and she was too tired for the words to be practised.

She wanted him; she'd proven it too often to count. And the way she snuggled against him now was far more womanlike than childlike. 'Whose money did you spend today, Jazmine?'

Even the lifted hand couldn't cover the massive yawn. 'Don't worry, Your Cranky Highness, it wasn't your future I gave away. Grandfather and I have a private account we started after Orakis's last attempt to kill us. It's our own money that we use when we run out of government funds.' She kicked off her hated shoes as she spoke; her legs curled up on the seat and her head fell to his chest, breathing slow and even.

She gave away her own money to help others—as did the old man he'd thought of as an autocrat, someone who lived the palace life while others suffered.

Obviously, his first impressions had been far from right.

He used to think of himself as a pretty decent guy—but he'd never known himself until the past two weeks.

She felt like a trusting kitten, curled up against him. He watched her sleep, with curious warmth in his chest. He hadn't had this feeling with a woman before. He liked women, had been entertained by them, wanted them, made love if they were willing. He'd even flirted with the notion of being in love once or twice, but he'd always run from the notion of permanence. It was always a 'one day' proposition, a 'when the right one comes I'll know' belief.

Now 'one day' was here—but whether Jazmine was the right one or not didn't matter. This was his future; *she* was his future. It was take on the job or live with the regret that he could have helped change the world for the better, could have improved the lives of millions of people, and hadn't.

Jazmine's choice, or Hobson's, it had become his own. And with this complex and fascinating woman curled up in his arms and over his body, with one gentle kiss that hadn't even deepened to passion, he knew he'd found, if not the right one for him, then the unforgettable one.

When she moved against him, seeming uncomfortable, he pulled her onto his lap, cradling her. Just to let her sleep. Nobody needed to know.

She sighed and snuggled against his chest.

It had been a long, emotional day, and he still had his meeting with the king, to discuss his impressions of the day and what needed to be done. His eyes drifted shut, thinking of possibilities, dreaming of a future for the brave and strong people he'd just left, feeling the warmth of a woman's sleeping trust, believing in his honour and strength.

A passing rider on a motorbike lifted his digital camera and snapped a shot.

'Jobs, education, wealth—the words are used like political footballs these days. Jazmine says the other villages she's been to are much like Helmanus—in desperate need of something more immediate.' Charlie was pacing the room as he tossed his opinions at Grandfather like little bombs. 'The people I saw today are villagers living a traditional life. They don't *want* Western notions of what's best.'

'You know this, because…?' the king asked, far more delicately than Jazmine would have believed only yesterday.

'I speak Hellenican Greek, sire. Not quite the type they do near the Albanian border, but we communicated well enough,' Charlie replied, with respect tempered by leashed impatience. 'They want what they've always had: autonomy. Self-determination under the umbrella of the monarchy.'

'Which means?' Grandfather's voice was rich with hidden amusement, seeing what Jazmine did: that Charlie, in his pacing, was talking as if to himself and making plans in front of them for the well-being of her people.

Were they becoming his people too?

'Their own carpenter, plumber, cobbler and dressmaker. Their own water supply—and they need electricity reinstalled, stat. Running their own farms with their own sheep, goats and chickens, and eggs and fresh milk—growing their food the traditional way, not buying it at a super-market. And they definitely need firefighting ma-terials and a resident firefighter as well as a policeman.'

'How are we to accomplish this?'

Jazmine noted Grandfather had not called Charlie by his royal name, Kyriacou, once during this conversation. He'd done nothing to jerk Charlie from his thoughts and plans for Hellenia, just as he hadn't after Charlie had reported on his meeting with the Spanish ambassador—a meeting where he'd stunned Jazmine with his grasp on international affairs and his ability to stop the diplomatic tap-dance with words to get to the heart of the matter. She'd seen the ambassador's respect for Charlie deepen with every passing minute as well.

Jazmine smiled, watching him. Charlie was earning his own respect, forging his own path, his way.

'The village tradesmen are worn out, working day and night for little pay to make the houses liveable. They need apprentices for all trades, but can't afford to pay them, and the young men and women who want to learn can't afford to do so for nothing. They're the ones leaving the villages under Orakis's promise of something to do, right? I was thinking, if there was a government-run apprenticeship scheme—such as they have in Australia but on a bigger scale—it would bring wealth to the villages faster, it would mean extra hands for the needed work and keep the young people home.'

'Jobs, education and wealth,' Grandfather said softly, with a smile.

Arrested by the words, Charlie swung around to face the king...and slowly grinned. 'I suppose so, sire.'

'Within the boundaries of what my people are comfortable with. You're right. However, the cost of such a scheme—'

'If we start with what the nation can afford, sire—instigate the scheme in a few villages until they're autonomous or on the way to it—their taxes could be reinstated and used to fund the next few villages. And, as for the firefighting, we have a resident on tap. I could advise on what to buy, what buildings to use, even run classes if that's allowed.'

Grandfather blinked, his brows lifted. 'A fireman and closet economist at once?'

Jazmine kept her mouth closed. If Grandfather wanted to praise Charlie, she wasn't about to interfere.

Charlie's grin grew, but he wasn't accepting the praise. 'I always liked maths and economics at school. Their problems have simple solutions; it's just following the equations.' He shrugged. 'People have always been the harder thing to understand.'

'You've shown little hesitancy and great decision on how to help the people of Hellenia today.'

Charlie waved it off. 'Problems to do with money usually have an easy solution—if you have the funds for it?' He gave the king an enquiring look.

Grandfather bowed his head. 'I was wondering when you'd reach this point.'

They discussed the economy, the funds available and where to start. Charlie discussed how much it would cost with great vigour, but backed off from decisions on where to instigate the scheme first, claiming the king would know far better than he in which village or area they ought to begin.

At the innate respect it implied, Grandfather smiled at Charlie and gave the regal nod of approval. His covert glance at Jazmine also held approval—and a touch of relief.

Jazmine felt a warm glow. Her grandfather was too ill to hold the reins of government much longer. If he could hand over some of the heavier burdens to them this way, one at a time, Grandfather could rest easier with less on his mind. And Charlie, with his compassion, his mathematician's brain and eye for detail, would take on those jobs. He'd become a regent without even realizing it.

'Very well,' Grandfather decreed. 'I'll call a meeting of my ministers for tomorrow. You both are invited to attend. Thank you, Kyriacou.'

'I've suspended his classes for the next week or more, Grandfather.' Jazmine spoke for the first time. 'Charlie needs to know about Hellenia and its needs far more than the other education, which he can learn in time.'

'Well done, Jazmine.' Grandfather smiled at her. Ecstatic, she felt a silly grin curving her mouth.

Then she saw Charlie's eyes narrow as he stood silently, watching them.

With awareness of undercurrents that had always made him hard to deceive, Grandfather looked at them both and spoke regally. 'You are both excused.'

In an accord with Charlie she was far from feeling, she dipped down to a curtsey at the same moment he bowed. She felt the irony in both.

'He never gives a reason for sending anyone away, does he?' Charlie asked, almost conversationally; but she knew better, could feel the tension in his body, the heat of hidden anger.

'He doesn't need to. Why are you angry?' she asked bluntly.

He gave a swift glance around to the line-up behind them. 'We want to spend time in the gym. Sweep it now, and then turn off the intercom system. Don't turn it back on unless there's an emergency.'

'Certainly, Your Highness.' The minders turned and, speaking into their mouth-mikes, discreetly vanished.

'I don't do public scenes,' he informed her shortly when they had all gone.

She bit her lip over a smile she couldn't hold in.

She felt the slight relaxing of his muscles, the anger dissipating just a little. 'Okay. I *rarely* do public scenes,' he allowed with a reluctant grin. 'Wait until Candid Camera's switched off downstairs.'

He didn't touch her as they walked together, but she felt the heat, the intensity of him, as if he'd run his fingers over her skin. Everything felt sensitized, alive, tingling with awareness. After the kiss last night—this morning—she'd been aware of everything he did today, his every movement and nuance of feeling. When he'd lifted her into his lap, light and warmth had filled her, even in all those hidden places inside she'd thought would always be dark and cold.

He'd cuddled her. Not sexually, not aroused— just *holding* her.

They reached the gym, and Charlie smiled and swept his hand to the doors. Within moments, the room was empty of everyone but the two of them. 'So.' His arms folded over his chest. It would have been intimidating but for the memory of this afternoon: her head resting there, awaking to the reassuring warmth of his skin, the soft thud of his heart beneath her ear. She'd felt so *safe*. Just as she'd felt when they'd kissed. Instead of devouring her, he'd *cherished* her.

Jazmine had had visions of their first kiss, and he'd shattered them all. Expecting him to take her body and soul by storm, he'd crept quietly into her heart and taken it.

Just like that. She'd felt like Sleeping Beauty, waking up after a long sleep. She'd come to life, for the first time in so long she could barely remember.

There was such tenderness hidden beneath the shell of this reluctant prince who wanted to appear hard and uncompromising.

'What's the deal, princess?'

Lost in the gentle memory of his tenderness, she started at the harshness of the question, but clicked right back into action. Harshness and demand she was used to; she had armour against that. 'I don't understand.'

He sighed. 'Let's not play games. I'm too tired.' When she didn't answer, his face turned cold. 'The looks. The grins I saw just now. You and the old guy are up to something. I want to know what it is.'

'Oh.' Hot colour flooded her face; she could feel it running rampant across her skin, and ducked down a little, trying to hide it. 'That.'

'Yes, *that*.' He angled his face so she had to look at him again.

Humiliation crept over her soul. She turned away again. 'It was…private.'

'So you're saying it had nothing to do with me?'

The blush grew furious, and, with it, anger to match his. 'Not everything is about you,' she snapped.

'Attack is the best form of defence, they say. Good show, princess.' He took her arm—so tenderly, she barely felt it, it wasn't force—and turned her back to face him. 'A shame it's not convincing me.'

'I don't have to convince you,' she mumbled. *Oh, treacherous body, rebel heart!* One touch and she was trembling, melting, turning from princess to woman…

'Jazmine.' The name was beautiful as ever on his lips, those wonderful 'kiss me' lips. 'That's not the best start for us, if we're going to spend our lives together.'

And he drew her against him. Winning by dangling what she needed most before her, and by the most tender of seductions.

Even knowing it, still her head touched his chest, and she breathed him in: heated, spicy male. Still her hands touched his waist.

Still she melted.

'Cheat,' she whispered, breathing in and out. Breathing him.

He chuckled, and dropped a kiss on her hair. 'Street smarts, *loulouthaki*.'

Though it was nearly dark, summer light and warmth flooded her being with the nickname.

'Tell me, Jazmine. Trust me, *loulouthaki mou*,' he whispered into her hair. She shivered to her soul: *my little flower*.

'He...he smiled at me, Charlie,' she murmured into his skin. Afraid to look up as she bared that shivering soul. 'He hasn't smiled at me like that, since...'

There was a long, gentle silence while he waited, and she gulped and tried so hard not to let her eyes sting.

'Since I survived the meningococcus and Father and Angelo didn't. Since he lost his heirs and was stuck with only me,' she finished in a tired whisper. 'He's all I have. And today, he—he *smiled* at me.' She gulped again. 'He hasn't been proud of me from that day until today.'

And then years of repressed emotion broke open, and she cried. Cried on that sturdy warm chest with the heart beating as steady as his nature. He didn't speak, didn't pull away, just held her, releasing her hair from its confines and caressing the curls.

When she slowed to a series of most ungraceful hiccups, he lifted her face and wiped her tears with his sleeve because, being Charlie, he could carry her from a burning building or choke while he gave a child his air, but he didn't carry a handkerchief.

She sniffed and smiled up at him through the awkward actions of his arm, and wondered if there hadn't been a day in her life when she hadn't been waiting for him.

Though she'd denied it to him at first, she knew the truth. Throughout her lonely childhood and the most turbulent days of her life, she *had* pictured a prince coming along: a man willing to share her starved and smothered life and make her happy. She'd pictured him rich and handsome, a suave dancer and popular with everyone, knowing her world and able to overcome any obstacle with grace and style.

She'd been a silly, ignorant girl with all her imaginings, because she hadn't known better. Her visions of perfection were too much, and yet so much less than she needed, because they had never been of Charlie—her rough-diamond action-hero prince with a foul temper and a heart of pure gold.

'You know, when Lia feels down she and Toby always bake something.' He bent and kissed her nose, and it melted her heart more than any passionate merging of lips could have—though she wanted that, ached for it. But this tenderness from a man like Charlie undid her.

She smiled, feeling like an idiot but unable to stop. 'I think the chefs would have a fit if we went in and made a mess in their domain.'

He shrugged. 'So we wash up and put away. They won't know a thing.'

She stared at him, wondering if her jaw had dropped.

A chuckle burst from him. 'Don't tell me, princess, you've never washed a dish in your life?'

Embarrassed, she shrugged. She'd boarded at the best houses during her school years, with a companion, a bodyguard and a maid. She'd never made a bed, or washed or folded anything. Even minor royals in Hellenia had fully-equipped houses with an artillery of servants to see to their every need. It was generational employment; her servants' parents had served her parents, and so on. They were part of the family.

But what they did for her, and how they did the same work day after day, had always been as much a mystery to her as running the nation would be to them.

'Then it's my turn to teach you something.' With another laugh at her obvious disbelief that he wanted to teach her to wash up, he murmured against her mouth, 'Don't worry, *loulouthaki*, it's not rocket science. I'll be with you through the ordeal. You'll see—it'll be fun, just you and me, cooking, feeding each other…'

Mesmerized by the picture he painted by his touch, she nodded. She didn't pretend to herself that when he spoke so caressingly, touching her mouth with his, she wouldn't go to the ends of the earth with him.

'I'll meet you there tonight, when everyone's asleep.'

A late-night assignation with her prince… How could she resist? 'I'll make sure the cameras are turned off.'

His face didn't darken at the mention of the intrusions into their private life. He grinned and drew a finger down her nose, and her whole body heated in reaction. 'It's a date.' He winked at her, and strolled away. 'Oh, and wear something you can make a mess in, because I plan to muss you up good.'

Warmth filled her entire being at the words

she'd never heard before. He was like sunlight and rain to her dried, parched soul, lost too many years in rules and appearances.

It was time she was just a normal woman.

# CHAPTER NINE

CHARLIE and Jazmine surveyed the steaming, lumpy disaster in front of them with varying amusement and disgust.

'Is that how it's supposed to look?' Jazmine asked dubiously.

He made a rueful face. 'It never looks like that when Lia and Toby do it. They've had years' more practice, I guess.' Until now, he'd merely watched sport and waited, or watched them cook with a grin. They did it so flawlessly—except when Toby tossed a bit of flour in Lia's hair, and she'd rub something else in Toby's hair...

Hmm; smearing cake on Jazmine's mouth, and kissing it off... What a glorious vision.

'So we made all this mess—' she swept her hand around the assembled riot of egg shells, cocoa and sugar, spilled milk and flour '—for nothing?'

'Never!' Determined now, he grabbed a spoon

and dug it into the dark confection. 'Get the ice cream, princess.'

'So I'm "princess" again now?' She twisted her face to grin at him. 'What did I do to deserve that slam?'

He stared at her, unable to suppress the grin. 'Nothing; you're right. Your hair's a mess, your poor old Oxford T-shirt is covered in flour, and you have a big smudge of mixture on your cheek.'

'I do?' She began scrubbing at her face.

He laughed then. 'Three or four smudges, actually. I should know—I put 'em there.' *With his hands, while kissing her.*

'Well, take a look at yourself!' she retorted, pointing to a mirror in the hallway just outside the kitchens. 'Your shirt's half-undone, you've got stuff in your face *and* your hair, and you have smudge on your...'

Her blush delighted him. 'On my what?' he whispered near her ear.

She was all rosy now, and barefoot, with her ratty old T-shirt hanging over her silky tracksuit pants, and her hair carelessly pulled back with a few pins with chocolate and flour all over, she looked adorable.

How had he ever thought of her as untouchable? He could barely keep his hands off her. And she loved every touch. They'd kissed every thirty seconds while cooking—which had been the cause of this cake mess. He'd been too busy kissing her to put on the timer, and, when he'd finally remembered, he'd had to guess.

'On your chest...and stomach. There.' She pointed to a half-dried gloop of mixture across his shirt.

'Ah, that explains the smudge on your shirt, just a few inches higher.' He nodded wisely as he pulled her towards him. 'Ah, see? A perfect match. You think you gave it to me, or me to you? Because that last kiss got pretty—'

'Ice cream,' she interrupted in a laughing, would-be firm voice, and she slipped out from under his arms to run to the freezer. 'Here we go,' she announced as she took another spoon and scooped ice-cream on their messy attempt at cake. 'A veritable feast!' Grinning, she lifted the spoon he'd stuck in the cake and handed it to him. It had slimy bits of uncooked cake on it. 'Lucky it has loads of sugar.' She took a scoop into her mouth. 'Mmm...taste it, it's good.' She beamed at him. 'My first cake!'

He couldn't move. He didn't want cake, he wanted her. She was small and sweetly de-lectable, his own private feast, and he wanted to dine on her night and day, day and night, until he was ready to move on.

*Oh, yeah, and when's that going to be? Face it, Costa—you're hooked.*

He ignored the voice in his head. He'd fancied himself in love before and had tired of the girl or woman in question usually within a few weeks. This wasn't love, it was infatuation with the kind of woman every man fantasized about but knew was out of his reach. He had a little time left to get her out of his system.

*If it's going to happen,* the voice taunted him, *especially since you're not leaving, and you know it. Jazmine is your future.*

'Charlie?'

*Char-rr-liee.* Ah, he was addicted to the way she said his name. Whenever she said it, he had to kiss her.

'I'd rather taste you,' he said huskily, and bent to take smears of the confection from her mouth with his tongue. 'Mmm, delicious,' he murmured, and kissed her again, deep and warm and getting hotter by the moment.

'Ah, Charlie, *Charlie,*' she murmured between kisses more delicious than any food could be—the touch of her hands roaming his body, the sweetest thing he'd ever known. 'Ah, what you do to me…'

'*Loulouthaki,*' he muttered back, kissing her over and over, shaping her form with his hands so their bodies fit perfectly together. 'I can't stop. Not touching you, not thinking about you. I've got to be with you.' Roughly, he whispered in her ear, 'In my bed, Jazmine. I want to make love to you so much I'm burning inside.'

'Me, too, Charlie, me too.' She kissed his throat, and he shuddered with need, longing, whatever the hell it was that made him feel scorched from the inside out when she wanted him this way— when she only looked at him like that, his shining-eyed, dishevelled angel. From the cool, mysterious Mona Lisa she'd become a flower with her face to the sun, and it happened when she was near him.

'She comes alive when she sees you, Charlie,' Lia had said last night, in their usual fifteen-minute talking ritual before bed. And she'd gone on, 'And so do you.'

Alive? More like *burning* alive, and never more so than right now.

'Let's go,' he whispered, cupping her breast with his palm, feeling her shiver and arch up to him.

The sweet fire in her eyes became urgent. 'Where? Where can we go, Charlie?'

And just like that reality returned. There was

nowhere. He couldn't make love to her in his room or hers without the entire palace knowing; he couldn't take her to the forest. She deserved better than a tumble in the grass, and not because of her title.

He swore to himself, and blew out a sigh. 'Sorry, *loulouthaki*.' He gathered her close, stroking her hair. 'I shouldn't have let things go so far.'

Breathing harshly with as-yet uncontrolled desire, she nodded against his chest. 'I wish—I wish things were easy for us, Charlie.'

He heard the welter of emotions in her voice— the yearning, the regret—and, though he was aching too, wishing they could just have the right to choose to be lovers without consequences of international proportions, he forced himself to say, 'The things most worth having don't come easy.'

She smiled up at him as though he'd said something wonderful, as though *he* was wonderful, and his heart pumped so hard he was finding it hard to breathe. 'You think we're like that? We're "something worth having"?'

Oh, those shimmering eyes, they'd cast some sort of enchantment over him. Her sweet, sweet face, and the lips he couldn't resist! They were arranged against him now in a mysterious woman's battle-formation, and he didn't have the weapons for the fight. He couldn't take that glow from her eyes, coming straight from a heart as beautiful as it was, denied the simple things that made her so happy.

'I think we could be, Jazmine. I do.' Unable to stop himself, he kissed her once, twice, tasting light and magic. 'If everything else weren't in the way.'

She pulled away then, the light in her eyes dimmed. 'Yes.' The word was thick, forced. 'Everything else.' She turned to the counter. 'The ice cream's melted into the cake. It's inedible now.' She turned back to him with a would-be smile. 'So, now are you going to show me how to clean up as expertly as you taught me to bake a cake?'

The pain he'd tried so hard to avoid was there in her stiff stance, in the way she wouldn't look at him as she smiled. 'Would you rather I lied to you?'

After a moment, she said huskily, 'No. Would you rather I cried on you again, or begged you to stay to take on a country still in turmoil for my sake?'

Honesty forced him to admit it. 'No.'

She nodded, as if she'd expected it. 'Then leave it. We had a good time—now let's clean the mess we've made.'

He had the feeling she wasn't talking about the dishes.

Defeated, he turned to the sink and took their ruined cake, scraping it into the bin. It seemed symbolic. 'I'll rinse everything before putting it in the dishwasher. You want to clean down the counters and put the food away while I stack up?'

When she nodded, he handed her a clean cloth and a bottle of anti-bacterial spray he'd found in a cupboard earlier. She took them with quiet thanks: the perfect princess covering the hurting woman.

Hurting meant she liked him…had feelings for him.

He'd been so stupid. The protected princess—always accompanied, always in an emotional ivory-tower where everything she did and said was right—knew so much more about running a country than he did. She knew about pain and loss, protocol and manners, what to give to people, and when. But, when it came to the kind of world he'd lived in, she was completely innocent. She didn't know *how* to play the field and walk away afterwards with a smiling goodbye, lying if necessary to keep pride intact. She'd been too busy all these years doing the right thing for her family, for her people.

And he'd played with her, teased her, flirted with her; had touched and kissed her when she'd been receptive.

But he'd forgotten the essential difference between Jazmine and those women: they knew the game. If they got hurt, they went home, ate chocolates and bitched to their girlfriends, hated him for a while, then met someone else. They moved on.

Jazmine couldn't move anywhere. She couldn't eat chocolate for long without the press making a fuss about her weight or zit-outbreak. She couldn't play around with a guy or get dumped without it making international headlines. And, if Charlie was her type of guy, how was she going to meet another one? It wasn't as if he could get one of his firie mates over here and set her up.

Bloody hell. He'd stuffed it up again. He had to fix this somehow.

She wouldn't look at him, and answered his comments so briefly he gave up after a while. But the silence in which they worked, after the teasing, laughing and kissing before, grew unbearable. Damn it; how could he miss her when she was right here?

'I'm going to bed,' she said when they were done. 'Thank you for coming with me today, for letting me sleep…and for the cooking lesson.' A smile flitted across her face and was gone.

She was looking at him, but not *at* him—as if he'd turned transparent, and she was seeing through him.

He couldn't let her go like this. As she passed, he grabbed her arm. 'Jazmine…'

She didn't struggle or ask him to let go, as most women he'd known would have. She simply turned and looked at him, her smile remote.

A hurting Mona Lisa, trying to hide her pain but not knowing how, apart from resorting to the disguise she'd always used. But now he could see through it, see to her clear, sweet heart and soul.

'Hell, princess, I'm sorry,' he grated through an aching throat. 'I've been here two weeks and I've failed you.' He swore, feeling more of a jerk than he ever had before. 'I don't know what it is— wrong timing, wrong guy— Well, hell, we all know that,' he admitted with a strange, bitter-sweet tang. 'You're not to blame, you're perfect.'

'Stop it!' she cried, wrenching her arm from his grasp. Startled, he looked at her, and saw tears splashing on her cheeks, dashed away. 'You think *you're* a failure after two weeks? I've failed all my life! I've spent my life at boarding schools, finishing schools and top universities—places I didn't want to be, studying subjects pertaining to a job I never thought I'd have. I wasn't allowed to cry at my mother's funeral because of the stupid cameras. I was *seven*. I couldn't cry when Father and Angelo died. I've never been allowed to swear or yell, or say anything out of place. And, now I'm Princess Royal, I work fourteen- to sixteen-hour days, and am expected to look perfect the next day when I rarely get more than four hours' sleep a night. I don't want this job, either, Charlie!'

Her voice wobbled as she dashed at her eyes again. 'But, if I don't do it, who will? Can you blame me for hoping you'd want to share the job, make the best of it together? Now that's gone too, and I *hate* you for it!'

Shocked into silence before her first sentence was complete, Charlie dropped his hands and stared at her—all of her. Finally the composure had, not cracked, but broken; the real woman stood before him. He'd never heard her use so many words about herself; it had always been as if she didn't matter compared to the needs of others. He'd felt so inadequate in his selfish wish for a private life. She'd seemed so...perfect.

Now he knew the truth, and— Ah, hell, he admired her more than ever for being human, im- perfect and fragile beneath the flawless façade, and doing her best anyway. Liked her, admired her, wanted her, and it was all woven together in a tangled thread.

And, like the woman of courage and integrity

she was, she didn't run off but stood in front of him, panting a little, and waited for him to answer.

If only he knew what to say. If he banged his thick skull against the wall, would the right words come?

He had to say something, anything. Eventually he gave up and let words come whether they were right or wrong. 'Yeah, thank God, she's human after all.'

Could he have said anything worse? Was he so determined to destroy this? In two minutes he'd turned a peaceful, happy situation to crisis point with his stupid mouth.

She was staring at him as if half his brain had wandered off without his noticing. 'Is that all you can say? I said I hate you!'

'I want to kiss your tears away,' he blurted, and wanted to run off to find wherever his brain had disappeared. He closed his eyes. 'Sorry. I don't know what to say, except thank you for trusting me with your secrets, *loulouthaki mou.*'

'But I'm not your little flower, Mr Costa. I'm not anything of yours at all.'

The words were cool and distant. He opened his eyes to see her opening the door to the long hall and stairs to the main quarters. 'Jazmine!'

Being Jazmine, of course, she turned back. That

was his *loulouthaki*, so strong, so beautiful, he ached. She said nothing, just waited.

Words came from nowhere, words he didn't know were in him until they'd reached her. 'Don't give up on me. This is a hell of a decision and I can't make it based on the fact that I like you, that I respect you, can't stop wanting to touch you, or wanting to be with you. That kind of thing doesn't always last a lifetime.'

'It doesn't always end in disaster, either,' she said quietly. 'And it isn't me giving up on you, Charlie. You're giving up on yourself.' She looked in his eyes as she threw her bomb in exchange for his. 'I suspect you've been giving up on yourself from the time Lia got sick until now.'

Now he was truly stunned. *She knew he'd let Lia down when she'd needed him most.*

He felt disaster coming and didn't have a clue how to stop it. He was unable to retaliate because he knew she fought her weaknesses, this woman who was every inch the princess, even with her shirt hanging out, chocolate smears on her face and lips thoroughly kissed.

'You know it's true.' She looked deep into his eyes as she kept tearing apart the fabric of his self-delusion—that beneath the hero there was a sham who hadn't been able to save his parents or his sister. 'Something tells me that if you give up on yourself this time, whether you decide to be Charlie Costa, fireman, or Kyriacou Charles Costa Marandis, you'll regret it for life.'

The rightness of what she said was like an electrical current racing through him, and still he couldn't move.

'I'm not giving up on you, Charlie, because I believe in you. I believe you can do anything you put your heart and soul into. I believe you can do this. And, if you end up leaving, I'll believe Hellenia has lost the best king she could have had.'

And then she was gone, and the passionate conviction of true belief hung in the air behind her.

She knew—knew almost the worst of him—and she still believed.

He strode down the long hall and up the stairs after her, taking three at a time to reach her; but this time he didn't have to grab her or call. She heard him coming and turned back, on the second-to-top stair. Still. Waiting.

'That's not it,' he grated harshly, hating himself, hating her for making him say the words he'd kept dammed up for eleven years, words he'd never told Papou or Yiayia, words he hadn't even slurred to Toby on their drunkest nights. 'You don't know it all.'

Her eyes gentled, for no cause he could find. 'Then tell me, Charlie. Make me understand why you're so sure you'll fail me and fail my country.'

He didn't stop to move or think; he had to say it now, or he'd take off and never come back. 'You seem to think I'm some paragon because I happened to be in a position to save a child—'

'Don't forget the other fifty-three people you saved too,' she said softly, those eyes shimmering again.

He had to stop it!

'Yes. I hate myself because I let Lia down,' he snapped as if it was her fault. 'She collapsed and I freaked out. I didn't know what to do if I couldn't force feed her. All I could see was my sister dying in front of me, that she had been for months, and I hadn't even *noticed*.'

DEFCON 4. Sirens were screaming in his head: *Stop; stop here*! But he couldn't.

'This within a year of your parents' death and in your first year as a fireman?'

He waved that off; it was no excuse. 'Do you have any idea how much I love her? She's my sister, my family, she's everything—and I didn't know what to do. Toby took over, did everything that was my place to do. He was with her day and night around his schedules. They let him stay because he was healing her. I just made her feel worse about being so sick, for scaring me like that. I hated my sister because she might die and leave me alone!'

There; surely she'd hate him now for being the selfish jerk he was—and if she left now, he wouldn't have to.

'So you understood why I said I hated you.' Her voice was so gentle, so filled with sympathy, he felt sick.

He couldn't look at her as he conceded, 'Maybe—but we've known each other two weeks. You can hate me for life and it doesn't matter if I'm not here. Lia is my sister, my *family*, and I hated her until the day she came out of the clinic!'

Surely it was over now? *Please, please just be disgusted and leave now...*

After a long silence, she said, a wealth of under-standing in her voice, 'Was it Lia you hated, Charlie? Or was it the fear that your beautiful, wise, lovable sister might die and leave you alone in the world? So, being only eighteen, you ran away whenever you could—and now you think it's inevitable. Your Papou ran away too—it has to be genetic. The men in your family can't measure up.'

*Click.*

# CHAPTER TEN

As IF she'd flicked on a switch inside him, he felt the defusion of all his anger in an instant. She'd found the truth without ten years of searching for it. How did she do it?

He didn't answer. He couldn't. Couldn't she see the truth—that he wasn't worthy, no matter what she hoped? But she was still here, still fighting for something only one of them believed in.

'That's still not it.' God help him, he felt his voice going; he had to force the ending out. The words to destroy her sweet faith, and make her see the man he really was. 'The night my parents died, I was supposed to pick them up from a party. I said, sure, I'll come for you—but I was on a date with the girl I'd liked for months, and turned off my phone. I didn't want any interruptions. I figured they'd get a taxi if Dad had been drinking.'

He couldn't go on. He was shaking and cold, so cold, going back to the night that had defined his life, a night he'd buried in the blackness of a memory he couldn't bear to revisit. He only did so now because eight million lives were at stake…and the happiness of one special princess.

'Charlie…'

He felt her coming down the final two stairs to him, her hands reaching out to him. His eyes snapped open. 'Don't touch me.' *I don't deserve it.*

Her hands fell. 'Go on, then,' she said quietly.

'When I didn't show up they did get a taxi— and they were hit by a drunk driver.' Stark as it was, he couldn't stop there. 'They took hours to die, Jazmine. *Hours.* And because my phone was off Toby, Lia, Papou and Yiayia had to go to the hospital without me. It broke them. Yiayia never got over it. She got sick and died two years later. Papou went away inside. And Lia—' he looked at her, waiting for the disgust, the hate without flinching '—just stopped eating.'

This was it—disaster. The end of all things for them.

After a minute, maybe two, she asked, 'Did you get to the hospital…in time?'

He sighed and turned away. 'In time to hear my father tell me it wasn't my fault, and—and to look after the family. Mum—was gone.'

And he broke.

By the time the third gasping sob was torn from him, her arms were around him, drawing him to sit on the stair, and she sat on the one above, holding him, rocking him. She crooned nonsense words and held him and rocked him while eleven years of unspoken grief escaped from its cage, having held him hostage inside a half-life. He'd saved other peoples' loved ones because he hadn't been able to save the ones he loved. He'd spent years hiding from anything permanent or good because he believed he didn't deserve it.

He still didn't. But goodness and sweetness had come to him whether he was worthy or not, by the autocratic will of an old man who needed an heir, and a brave, stubborn little flower who believed in him no matter what he did or said, or how many times he failed.

'So that's why you ran from Lia's illness,' she whispered eventually, kissing his forehead, his hair. 'You were afraid you'd make her worse. It wasn't because you hated her. You loved her too much.'

Recognizing a truth he hadn't seen until she said it, he nodded. He was so tired, too tired even to ask the obvious question.

He didn't need her answer. It was clear she didn't hate him. But why she cared at all, why she was even still here, he had no idea. The inex-

haustible forgiveness that seemed to live inside
her would forever be a mystery to him. He sure
as hell couldn't find a way to forgive himself.

She said nothing else, and he was relieved.
Relieved she didn't give him the platitudes he'd
half-expected, the reassurances he wouldn't have
accepted. Strange that, after so little time
together, she knew him so well, better than
anyone, even Lia or Toby.

They sat there a long time, until he felt something approaching peace.

Relief, and peace. They were emotions foreign
to him for so long he'd forgotten how uplifting
they felt…and he'd found them from a source
he'd least expected.

'Come,' she said gently, after a minute or an
hour had passed on that stair. She dropped down
to whisper in his ear, 'I don't know about you,
guv'nor, but my bum's numb. Ain't got enough
fat to cover it.'

He choked on unexpected laughter at her off
cockney accent. 'Where did you get that from?'

She grinned at him, proud. 'British soaps. I went
to Oxford, remember. I lived in England for three
years. Did history, philosophy, religious studies
and political science. Very boring stuff.' She
yawned hugely, theatrically, making him almost

want to laugh again. When he didn't, she smiled and tugged at him until he stood.

He did so more to please her than anything else.

He let her lead him, not knowing where they went and not caring. He'd go where she wanted, would do what she asked... so long as it didn't involve destroying eight million lives and ruining hers.

When they reached his room, she opened the door and turned to the night sentries. 'This will not be reported to my grandfather. Not our time in the kitchen, nor anything you heard, nor my whereabouts for the rest of this night. Tonight remains between the four of us, or you will regret it. Is that clear?'

Despite feeling so numb, Charlie felt a brow lift. She was every inch the future queen, all five-feet-three of her the protective lioness. She was protecting *him*—and strangely, after eleven years of running a family, career and being his own man, it felt good to have someone take charge for a little while.

He wasn't surprised when the security pair nodded after hesitating a moment. 'Yes, Your Highness,' they both said, and bowed.

Jazmine flicked on the lights and walked into the suite with a regal step, a barefoot Queen of Sheba.

Enchanted by her in any mode, he followed and closed the door.

She'd closed the heavy curtains, shutting them off from security, from cameras and movement-sensors. Then she padded over to him, went up on tiptoe and kissed him softly. 'Charlie,' she whispered, her eyes shimmering, and pulled off her shirt, offering herself to him without constraints.

He'd thought his heart couldn't burst any further. He looked down at her in tracksuit pants and lacy bra, and her chocolate smears, moved beyond bearing because he knew it wasn't pity, tempted beyond almost all reason.

He forced a smile. 'You're beautiful, *loulouthaki*, and I want you so much...but tonight...' He turned slightly away so she wouldn't see the evidence that he was lying, lying for her sake, because he couldn't take this final gift from her. 'After all the confessions and crying—I don't think I can.'

It was the only excuse that had a hope of working.

When the silence stretched out and he felt her hurt, he gave her what he could, because touching her right now might have broken his will. 'I've never told anyone what I told you tonight, Jazmine. Eleven years...' His voice cracked; he made it happen. Even though what he said was truth, he needed to convince her, because one more moment and he wouldn't be able to say no. Aching and burning for her, his blood on fire and his mind and body screaming, he made himself stay still. For her sake.

'I'm so stupid.' He heard the rustling sound as she slipped on the shirt, and his body flayed his mind for holding onto its last principle. Then he felt her arms around his waist, her head resting on his arm. 'Let me stay until you're asleep,' she whispered, caressing his stomach until he was so brittle he thought he'd shatter.

With all his will, with everything he had, he nodded and forced a yawn.

His mother or Yiayia would have had a fit if they'd seen him fall to the bed still fully clothed; it was almost a cardinal sin in the family. But it was too dangerous to undress when his self-control was hanging by a thread and his lovely princess watched him with such tender hunger. What did she see in him? God help him, help them both, because this *had* to be all wrong, but it felt so damn right…

He felt her climb onto the bed beside him. He knew she'd take him in her arms before she did it. He didn't dare protest or move; he had to lie limp and pliant. One move and she'd feel his full-to-bursting arousal. The woman of his dreams was holding him in her arms and he could do nothing about it, because she was the one woman he could never have, could never deserve.

Eventually the peace he'd felt on the stairs returned, stealing into his soul, and he slid towards sleep; it robbed him of his will. He'd never remember what he said later.

'I think I'd have married you if you weren't a princess,' he mumbled.

Her tender laugh slipped inside his half-dreaming state, bound as he was by the impossible magic of being in her arms after all he'd told her. 'I think you will anyway, *prinkipas mou, vasilias mou.*'

*My prince. My king.*

And in that twilight between waking and sleeping—when anything could be possible, believing he was sleeping and it would all slip away in the realm of the unbelievable tomorrow—he believed her.

# CHAPTER ELEVEN

*A Fairy tale Come to Life: The Lost Prince
and Princess Found!*
*The Hero Who Won a Crown: From Fire-
Retardant Suit to Savile Row. Can He Save
Hellenia from the Flames of War and Win the
Heart of the Princess?*

FOLLOWED closely by his distraught sister, Charlie
stalked into the morning room and threw down
the wad of newspapers on the breakfast table.
'Did you do this?' he barked at the king, who was
placidly eating a boiled egg, fresh toast and tea.
Max sat beside him.

The king looked up, seeming pained. 'Must you
begin the day with dramatic demands? I'm an
old man. The heart isn't what it once was.'

Charlie picked up one of the tabloids and waved
it in the king's face. 'These were outside my room
this morning. Our lives have hit world headlines,

from Sydney to London and New York. There isn't a single paper or magazine that doesn't have our faces on it!'

The king shrugged with nonchalant elegance—a man who'd got his way. 'It had to happen, Kyriacou.'

'Not without help!'

'You're right.' The king smiled up at him. 'Your own. I merely provided details. By handing Jazmine into the car with that, uh, affectionate look on your face, and by allowing her to sleep in your lap in the car as you did, you started the fire.'

Dumbfounded, he stared at the king. 'What did you say?'

With a smile, the king said, 'It was very romantic, I must say, but with the press around it was rather foolish if you wanted to continue remaining a royal mystery. A passing photographer snapped the shot and began digging. It didn't take long. I hear he got half a million for the story.'

Goaded by the self-satisfied look on the king's face, Charlie snapped, 'You don't have to be so damned smug about it. I can still renounce the title.'

'Theo Angelis,' Lia intervened, in soft rebuke. 'This has rightfully hurt and upset us. We've been trying our best to do everything you've asked, and now we feel as if you've repaid us with betrayal. Can you please tell us what happened?'

The lined old face softened, as it always did for Lia. 'I never betrayed you, Giulia. We knew nothing until the calls began coming in two days ago, asking for confirmation. When we were shown the shots, and told the captions—"love with the help"—our only option was damage control. We had to make the announcement of who you are, and announce the royal engagements, unless you both wished to be flooded with unwanted suitors from all over the world within days.'

'*We?*' Charlie asked, softly, dangerously, ignoring all the more noble reasons for the leak, and his own part in his downfall. He'd deal with that later. 'Two days ago?'

'The other person Grandfather means would be me.'

Charlie swung around to face the woman who'd so recently been in his bed almost all night. 'You did this? Two days ago?'

Seeming totally calm, Jazmine nodded. 'Yes, I did.'

He felt a muscle twitch in his jaw. 'Without telling me?'

'Yes.' Not a muscle moved in her face. Not a shred of guilt in her lovely eyes.

'Am I permitted to ask, Your Royal Highness, why neither of us were told about it? Why did Lia and I have to see these to find out what was going on in our own lives?' His voice dripped with anger and bitterness.

At that, Jazmine flicked a glance at his sister with a touch of anxiety. 'Lia, if we could have told you, warned you… I'm sorry. The story was going to come out, and—and Charlie, well—'

'Yes, we all know you weren't about to let me handle it, right? The back streets prince would have hit somebody or done something to embarrass the royal family.'

She looked at him and lifted a brow. 'We judged that you weren't ready to deal with the press frenzy at this point, Charlie.'

He snatched a tabloid at random and waved it in her face. 'Well, whether or not I'm ready, it's already here. If I'm not ready, I'll renounce the position. Orakis will be happy to take my place. He's probably getting the party ready as we speak.'

Jazmine whitened so fast he forgot why he was so angry. He dropped the paper, and took her by the shoulders to hold her up.

At the sweet magic of a single touch, the fury flooded right back. She'd kissed him, touched him, listened to his darkest secrets and slept in his bed, in his arms, when she'd already *betrayed* him?

Still, he marched her to a chair and forced her down into it. 'Head between your knees, princess. You look like you're about to faint.'

She kept her gaze on him, dark, wounded. 'Are you going to renounce the title and position?' She spoke barely above a whisper.

'You betrayed me!' he shot right back. 'You kissed me and slept in my bed, knowing you'd betrayed me and forced me into this!'

'She did *what*?' the king roared.

Ignoring her grandfather, keeping her gaze trained on Charlie alone, she nodded. 'It wasn't planned that way. That night was so—so perfect...' She sighed. 'Believe me, I am sorry for it, Charlie—but I had no choice. There was no other way.'

'There certainly is no other way now,' the king snapped. 'You will marry her, Kyriacou, and take the position, if you have had your way with her!'

Charlie, too, ignored the king; this wasn't his place or decision. 'Then I'm sorry too, princess.' He turned to the king then who, despite his anger, looked grey again, and older than his years. 'How long do I have before I have to make an announcement?'

The wrinkled old hands gripped the edge of the table. 'The press, the people, and Orakis will expect an announcement within a day or two, or our silence will confirm your position for you. And, if you agree to make the announcement, you must be trained with the correct words, either of acceptance or renunciation. The announcements on your weddings must come at the same time. Speculation's already rife, and we need heirs. If one isn't already on the way,' he added, with a touch of acid.

Ignoring that too, Charlie gave the king a curt nod. 'Then Lia and I have a lot of thinking to do. We need peace and space.'

'Weddings? Heirs?' A tiny, wobbling whisper sounded from behind him. 'No, oh no…'

Max came round to her and whispered something—probably, knowing Max, some reassurance that he was happy to wait—but this time it didn't work. Lia stared at Charlie, and he knew what he had to do.

He wasn't letting his sister down again. Ever.

'I want a phone, sire. My best friend's like family to us. He must be pretty cut up, finding out about us through the tabloids. We need to talk to him.'

'If you mean the Winder boy, he knows,' the

king said curtly. 'He's quoted as saying "no comment" in seven publications.'

Holding Lia's hand, Charlie met the old man's eyes and waited. He'd stated his needs. Repetition was a sign of weakness he refused to indulge in at this point.

Lia looked up at the king. 'I won't be rushed into marriage and babies with a near stranger to please you,' she said with quiet dignity. 'This is too big a decision for either of us to make without talking to the only person left in the world we consider family. So bring Toby here—or we'll go home to him.'

The king flinched at Lia's distant tone, which bordered on ice after over two weeks of warm wisdom and ready affection. After perhaps thirty seconds, he barked at a servant to bring a phone. 'I assume you both wish to discuss your pending decision with your friend?'

Charlie felt Lia nod at the same time he did.

'We can't risk your giving sensitive information over the phone. We've been betrayed that way in the past.'

'Find a way,' Charlie said, with that same soft danger. Not asking—telling. Demanding the king find a way to let them speak to Toby.

'This is the boy who helped Lia through the

anorexia ten or eleven years ago,' the king mused.
'He obviously knows how to be discreet.'

Again, they nodded.

'Call in Genevieve,' the king barked.

When the elegant, middle-aged senior attaché
arrived in the room, the king snapped, 'Contact
the embassy in Canberra. Have the prince and
princess's dear friend Toby Winder flown here on
the fastest possible jet, with no red tape. If anyone
has a problem, refer them directly to me.'

'Yes, Your Majesty.' Genevieve turned and left,
already dialling on her phone.

Charlie half-expected Lia to run to the king and
hug him, but she remained by his side. 'Thank you.
Toby's all we have. I won't do this without him.'

Tenderness filled the rheumy old brown eyes.
'Believe me, Giulia, no matter what your
decision is, you'll never be alone again. You will
always have us.'

Charlie felt an abrupt movement and turned.
Jazmine was leaving the room, her pace slow,
measured, which meant she'd lost her inner
equilibrium.

Without thinking it through, he strode to her
and took her arm. 'What's wrong? Besides everything that's already happened today, I mean,' he
added, mouth twisted.

Great, dark eyes looked up at him, lost. 'Please don't ask me. I can't tell you.'

She was shaking and trying so hard to hide it. Worried, he whispered, 'Come here.' He drew her close, holding her. 'Tell me, *loulouthaki.*'

He felt the negative shake of her head against his chest, almost infinitesimal. 'I—I can't. It wouldn't be fair.'

'To whom?'

'You,' she whispered. 'You've been forced into too much already.'

Moved despite his recent anger, he touched her hair and felt her shiver. 'So brave for such a small woman,' he murmured, tangled inside a web of tenderness, sweetness, honour, courage and sweet yearning—hers and his. 'Why isn't it fair to me?'

She looked up. Tears were shimmering in those haunting, haunted eyes. 'I've put you in enough chains. You—you might hate me, but you'd do the right, the honourable, thing. I—I can't do it to you.' Suddenly she went up on tiptoes, reached up and pulled him down to her, heedless of their watchers, and kissed him, quick and fierce. Fire flashed through him, but she pulled away before he could respond. 'I won't cry; I won't.'

She broke away from him and walked past the

security detail to the stairs, still slow and measured. Still lost and *broken*.

A single hand lifted when he moved to follow her, asking him to leave her be.

She'd locked him out, for his sake. He didn't have a clue what to do about it. He had a massive decision to make, and Jazmine's presence clouded his head and made him want what he still believed was unattainable.

Filled with a tempest of frustration, anger, sadness and something like regret, he turned back to the breakfast room. Max was talking softly to Lia, who had that distant-as-starlight look on her face again. She was withdrawing into herself.

Who did he rescue—Jazmine or Lia?

Lia looked at him and shook her head. She didn't want or need him to smother her. *Toby will be here tomorrow*, he thought to himself. *Toby always makes it right for her.*

He walked over to the king and said, 'Tell me what frightened her so much about my renouncing my title.'

Jazmine's grandfather searched his face for long moments.

'I need to know. She believes it will influence my decision, but make me hate her.' He waited, but the king didn't speak. 'Sire, I've been locked out of too many decisions regarding my life. If this affects me…'

'It doesn't affect you at all, if you renounce your position. It affects Jazmine only,' the king said slowly. 'That's what terrifies her.'

Lia broke away from Max and stood beside Charlie. 'Charlie's right. We need all the facts. We both care about Jazmine. Let us make the best decision for us all.'

After a moment, the king nodded. 'Spoken with your usual wisdom, my dear.' His eyes, when they turned to Charlie, were dark with the same kind of shot-fawn pain that had been in Jazmine's moments before. 'We forced the issue on you, and I'm sorry in one way. But it hasn't been just about naming a successor, or about royal weddings or heirs, or even settling the nation before I die—as important as all those things are.'

'Then what is it about?' Charlie asked quietly, dread creeping into his gut and making it churn. It was how he'd felt as he'd entered the burning house where the young mother had died: that somehow, no matter what he did, it wouldn't be enough.

The king took his glasses off and wiped them before he spoke. 'If you renounce your position, not only will Orakis take the throne when I die, the people will want a joining of both dynasties.' He replaced the glasses and met his eyes with a strange, dead look in them. 'Jazmine will be expected to become his queen, the mother of his children.'

Hot bile flew up from Charlie's gut without warning. Dear God. Jazmine... But Orakis wouldn't have her, not if he was alive to stop it.

There was only way he could stop it.

'Oh, can this farce get any worse?' he muttered to himself, turned on his heel and strode, not just out of the breakfast room, but right out of the summer palace.

He snarled and swore at the security detail that followed him. 'Get away from me. I'm not your prince...yet,' he added, the bitterness filling his entire soul.

*Yet.*

It was going to happen. *The unfit prince—step up to the podium, please, and do your duty...and try not to stuff it up again...*

If Jazmine had no choice, neither did he. If she was what she was, so was he. She was a princess, born and bred—and he was a stupid bloody hero-wannabe, a rough-edged, hot-tempered Joe from the back streets of Sydney who'd destroyed his own family. How the hell was he going to run an entire nation, and one already devastated by war?

He was going to fail; he had no doubt—but he

could no more leave a woman as beautiful and brave as Jazmine, with all the ability to shatter she kept hidden from the world, to Orakis's tender mercies, than he could have left that little girl to die.

Jazmine; lovely, courageous Jazmine had refused to tell him. She'd have gone to Orakis's bed rather than force Charlie to take a crown, a nation, and a wife.

He had no choice. If he walked away, Jazmine's fate would haunt him until the day he died.

Long, furious strides took him into the small, cool forest behind the palace grounds. He knew there were at least a dozen suits surrounding him as he walked, with their sunglasses, their ear-pieces and their guns.

Protecting their future prince, their future king. He knew it, and he knew they knew it. Everyone had known it all this time but him.

He turned and slammed his fist into a tree.

And, while Charlie accepted the inevitable and faced his future, King Angelis had his third heart attack in six months.

# CHAPTER TWELVE

*The next morning*

THIS time the royal family waited behind the protection of the massive oak doors of the country palace while the next enforced visitor from Australia arrived. The unofficial royals waited outside to greet Toby. They were dressed casually in designer jeans, Charlie in a polo shirt, Lia in a plain shift-top of creamy-lemon linen.

There was no fanfare for this arrival, no anthem or flag waving—and no privacy. At least forty cameras were trained through the gates to where the Rolls swept in.

From behind the long French windows leading to the balcony, Jazmine saw a massive bear of a man emerge from the Rolls, looking as raw and masculine as the man he claimed as best friend and brother. Toby Winder was all man from head to foot, with bronzed Aussie skin, streaky dark-

and-gold hair, and eyes like the Aegean Sea she could even see from this distance, they were so bright. A handsome face, bordering on craggy, with deeply grooved dimples she suspected many women would find irresistible.

He wasn't smiling now. He greeted his old friends from ten feet away, with a barely hidden hostility. Charlie and Lia moved towards him, slowly, as if pulled by magnets. Toby stared at them, every line of his face and body screaming silent betrayal.

Lia murmured something, ran to him, her arms open. His face softened; he opened his arms in turn, and she flung herself in, wrapping her arms tight around him.

After a moment's hesitation, Charlie took another step, and another. Toby Winder said something; Charlie grinned and gave him a rough hug and back thump.

And she'd thought brother and sister an unbreakable entity. This was a threefold cord she suspected no man could break.

Jazmine found herself biting her lip, worrying it on the inside.

'Don't worry,' Max said softly. 'He'll love you, Jazmine. Everyone does.'

She glanced at him, unable to hide her fear. Charlie hadn't spoken to her since she'd run off yesterday. He'd been avoiding everyone but Lia. 'If he doesn't— He's Charlie's best friend. What if he talks him—them—into going home?'

'Then we take off to Majorca and marry without permission. We'll find a way to make the people accept me as a suitable replacement—all we'd have to do is have a baby fast.' He tipped her chin up, making her look at him again. 'I know I'm not Charlie, but you really didn't think I'd leave you to Orakis, did you?'

Something inside her went mushy, filled with Max's caring and comfort. 'You're the best friend a girl could have.' She smiled at him, her eyes misty, but knowing it wouldn't happen. Orakis's growing support would make certain of it.

'The offer's only open, of course, if the fire-cracker prince doesn't come up to scratch—but I've seen the way he looks at you. I think *you're* his itch, and he definitely wants to scratch.' As she blushed, Max grinned at her. 'And you've become more than just a princess since he came. You're alive, and thinking of more than your duty. You're crazy about him, aren't you?'

She turned away. The words should be spoken to Charlie first…if he ever wanted to hear them.

Max squeezed her shoulder. 'Just remember, there's someone in your corner.'

Moved, she hugged his arm. 'I know, Max.'
She should always have known.

She didn't ask about his relationship with Lia;
she didn't have to. Charlie was right. There was
a sweet unconsciousness in Lia's eyes, no hint of
the woman, when she looked at Max.

But there were worse fates than marrying a friend.

Lia had squealed something and run to the
Rolls, emerging with a scruffy wad of fur…a
dog? She was petting it awkwardly with the hand
that held it, while hanging onto Toby. She
wouldn't let her friend go for a moment. And
Toby seemed to be making his friends smile and
laugh—but he kept swinging his gaze from
brother to sister with a half-hidden intensity
Jazmine sensed wasn't normal to his nature,
which showed how much these two meant to him.

Charlie, with a caution that sat foreign on his
shoulders, glanced at the eager press and said
something quietly to his friend. Toby nodded.

As one, the trio moved towards the house,
walking like a single entity.

They were up against a force to be reckoned
with. The rebel prince with a conscience and the
sweet, strong-willed princess had been challenge
enough when they'd joined forces—but with Toby
Winder in the equation they looked unbreakable.

Grandfather, still in bed after the minor attack—he'd be in bed for at least a week, and possibly would never leave that bed—would soon see what Jazmine did. She had to think of a way to make Toby see how much they needed Charlie and Lia to stay. She had to make him realize the stakes for her people.

No, the truth was that if she wanted Charlie and Lia to stay she'd have to give Toby Winder a reason to want to stay here in Hellenia—and she sensed that he was more like Charlie than he appeared. Toby Winder would give her yet another challenge, when she was already facing the challenge of her life.

'Your Majesty. It is an honour to meet you.' Toby bowed to the king, with the correct degree of respect.

The old king, with the back of the bed lifted so he appeared to be sitting—it helped his breathing as well as giving him an illusion of control—smiled and took Toby's hand. 'Welcome to Hellenia, Mr Winder, and to our home.'

'Please, call me Toby, Your Majesty. Nobody but banks and credit-collectors have ever called me Mr Winder.'

'Toby, then,' the king conceded. 'I hope you can

convince your friend to do the right thing for this country, and its people.'

'Lady Eleni told me what's at stake on the trip over—and why Charlie and Giulia could tell me nothing, Your Majesty.' Toby drew out Lia's real name with a perfect Mediterranean inflection— *Yoo-lya*—that made it sound almost as exotic and beautiful as Jazmine's. He'd always called her that, and he was one of a handful Lia would accept the name from. 'I hope I can be of help not just to my friends, but to you, and the country as well, sir. Hellenia's been through too much in the past five decades since Papou—eh, His Grace— left for Australia.'

Charlie watched the wily old fox melt under the sincerity in Toby's twinkling eyes and dimpled grin, and had to hold in the laugh. His friend always could charm the birds from the trees. Big and strong, safe and dependable, and a man of action, he still had the knack of making people believe everything he said. And, because he was dead honest and completely loyal, they were never let down either.

No man on earth had a friend like his. Toby was a man in a million.

Why hadn't it been Toby who'd fallen into this accident of birth? He'd make a brilliant king.

It was easy to see the king was thinking the same thing. Toby was a man secure in his place in the world. Everyone was smiling at him within a minute. Everyone loved Toby, always had and always would.

But then Lia's stupid mutt Puck escaped her half-hearted hold and began bolting, as was his wont. The crazy dog was marking new territory, and in the chase to catch him Charlie saw the king motion Toby over.

The look on his face when Toby answered whatever he was asked was grim and cold, and Toby looked quietly determined.

What on earth was going on?

Finally a servant grabbed Puck and took him outside to the royal kennels with the other dogs, and peace was restored…a smelly peace. A peace fraught with unexpected enmity between his best friend and the king.

Toby turned to meet Jazmine and Max. A tiny dart of darkness speared through his gut, watching Jazmine smiling at his best friend without the shadows he saw in her eyes when she looked at him. The doubt, the uncertainty, did not exist for her with Toby, and he had no idea if that was a good or bad thing.

He glanced at his sister. She was pale, looking

at her feet. He wondered what was going through her mind. Probably the magnitude of their decision, and what they could say to Toby when they were finally alone and in private.

As ever, his friend's uncanny attuning to Lia came to the fore. He turned from Jazmine with a smile, managing to accomplish turning his back on a princess without any lack of manners. 'Giulia, my beloved, to put it without any overkill, even jet food sucks. I've missed both you and your cooking like hell the past weeks. Therefore, I opine, it's way past the hour when we disappear to discover the royal kitchens and make some of your unbelievably delicious moussaka, and those decadent mud-muffins the way only you can make them...and we can talk.'

His sister really had changed. She took at least twenty seconds to look up, to smile—and, when she did, her eyes were filled with shadows.

Charlie had seen that look on her face before, but he'd never understood what it was. Not until he realized it was the same way Jazmine looked at him...

It struck him in the gut. Finally he knew Lia's secret, and only because he'd caught a single look, a moment. For the first time, he realized his sister was more than his little sister. She was a woman—a woman really stuck in a hellhole.

She was all but engaged to a stranger she liked—but the man she wanted was her best friend: a man whose birth completely precluded marriage to a princess.

Shocked at the thought of his sister as a sexual being in any way, he swung his gaze from her—and caught the expression on the king's face. The look he gave Toby was suddenly harder, more calculating. 'I think it's time we allowed these three to catch up.'

Charlie caught the look the king flashed at Jazmine and Max, who both nodded. 'We'll leave you,' Max said with a smile. Charlie stared at his new friend, narrow-eyed, but the look Max returned was bland.

'No, we'll go to my room,' Lia said, her voice a touch wobbly. 'No cameras.'

'That wouldn't be appropriate for a princess, my dear,' the king said, gently but with finality. 'Even such an old friend as Toby cannot enter your room.'

'I'll make sure the cameras are turned off in the tea room, and nobody will be at the balconies,' Jazmine said quietly. 'They can wait at the base of the stairs.'

The king nodded, looking exhausted by the five-minute audience. 'Well thought of, my dear.' He waved them all out.

The five young people left the king's sitting-room. When they reached the tea room, Jazmine and Max stayed only a minute to be certain orders had been followed. Then they wished them happy conversation, and moved to leave.

'Wait.'

At the command that sounded anything but peremptory—Charlie wished *he* had the knack of it—Jazmine turned back. 'Yes, Toby?'

'I won't be here under false pretences.' Not a muscle moved on Toby's face for a few moments. Everyone waited in silence, watching him, seeing the titanic struggle taking place inside the clearness of his eyes. 'Are the rumours true about the royal marriages for you—for all of you?' He stared hard at Max.

Taken aback by the directness of the attack from a man who'd been exquisitely polite and warm until now, Max nodded. 'It's the way things are done here. The king can't enforce it, but we all know we must do what's right for the country.'

'Then you need to know the true reason I'm here, besides advising my friends on what is best, not just for Hellenia but for them.' With the lightning-fast reflexes that made the big man such an amazing firefighter, Toby pulled Lia to him and kissed her. It was a bare moment's meeting of lips, but Lia's hand fluttered up to his chest and she kissed him back.

Charlie groaned. Hell, didn't he have enough to cope with without this? What the hell was Grizz up to?

Toby's eyes met Max's, filled with steely determination and open defiance. 'Whatever Charlie decides, I'll be doing my dead-level best to make Giulia choose to come home—with me. To become an ordinary firefighter's wife instead of making an alliance with you for the sake of power and wealth.' He stared at each of them in turn, keeping Lia in the curve of his arm. 'Nobody knows how to care for her and cherish her as I do. She's mine.'

Everyone in the room stood stock-still and gaped. Including the woman still lying in his arms.

Then with a gasped, *'How could you, Toby?'* Lia broke free of him and ran from the room.

'Giulia, wait!' Toby started after her.

But Jazmine grabbed his arm. 'No, don't. I'll go. You've done enough, Toby.' She ran after Lia.

And, while Max looked grim, Toby's bronzed face whitened.

'What the *hell* was that, Grizz?' Charlie demanded as soon as they were alone—after Max had followed the women in grim silence.

Toby's chin was still up, his eyes still glittering with fierce determination. '*That*, my friend, was a declaration of hostilities. The Winder version of rage against the machine—or, in this case, rage against royal power and privilege.' He sighed and muttered, 'More likely it's the rage against my own stupidity in not acting years ago.'

'English—preferably words of one or two syllables,' Charlie snapped. 'Look, mate, I know you don't want to lose us, I know you adore Lia—'

'No, you don't. You never knew.' Toby snarled right over him, startling him out of his attack. 'When it came to the relationship between Giulia and me, you've only ever seen what you wanted to see.'

Totally taken aback by Toby's unaccustomed ferocity, Charlie said quietly, 'So tell me what I haven't seen.'

Toby was pacing the room, his hands making a total mess of his thick hair. 'You might always have known I adore Giulia—but you've never known that I *adore* her.'

'Since when?' he gasped, stunned by what the words implied.

'Since we almost lost her,' Toby replied quietly. 'The day she collapsed, I knew she was my life.'

'But—but that was over ten years ago!' he gasped, unable to take it in.

Toby's mouth twisted wryly. 'Tell me about it.'

Charlie blinked again, unable to assimilate how little he knew of those he loved best. 'Ten years? *Ten years*, and you never once tell me you're nuts about my sister?'

His dearest friend in the world shrugged. 'It's the hardest place in the world to be, Rip. My best mate and his sister accepting me as family—and I couldn't look at her without...' He sighed, and grinned at Charlie a little ruefully. 'I don't suppose you want to hear that part.'

He'd barely heard it as it was. He still couldn't get over the sudden indigestion of information. 'Have you ever hit on her?' he demanded, wondering why it would bother him if Toby and Lia had ever got it on, or even if they did now.

*Now*, he thought wryly, *is the worst possible timing, worse even than mine and Jazmine's. At least I have the pedigree, some blue blood somewhere. Toby has nothing to offer against Hellenia's need, and Max's bloodline is impeccable.*

As if he'd heard Charlie's thought, Toby made a low, frustrated sound and looked out the window. 'No. There was a good reason—a damned good one—but now I wish to God I had…then I wouldn't be in this mess. I wouldn't be fighting a multi-millionaire duke, a king and a country—not to mention the carrot of fifty million euros—to keep the love of my life with me.'

A world of love and pain filled his dearest friend's voice. He hadn't even used the correct grammar, and Charlie, amazed as he was, couldn't help but respond. He put a hand on Toby's muscular shoulder with a rush of wordless empathy. The two friends stood that way for a few minutes, seeing the mirror of each other's lives in their situation. Both facing a battle beyond their ability and control, fighting uphill— Charlie to save a nation and a princess, Toby for the woman he loved.

Suddenly he wondered about the look on Lia's face—the same look he'd seen on Jazmine's. Did that mean…?

He shoved the thought aside. Even though he only had hours until he must make his announce-ment, right now wasn't about him. *Besides*, he added to himself, *I have no decision left to make.*

Eventually he said, 'You couldn't have had worse timing on this. The king had a heart attack last night. You can't make your intentions public.

If you did, and anything happened to him, Lia would never forgive you. She loves him like she loved Papou.'

Toby sighed, his eyes bleak. 'You've changed—both of you. Coming here has done something to you.'

Charlie shrugged. 'It had to happen—but Lia likes the changes, Grizz. She's slipped into the role of princess as if she was born here. You should hear her talk about her pet interests—the laws on divorce, and the needs of widows and orphans. You'll have a hell of a job convincing her to go home. She's needed here.'

'I can see that.' Toby spoke with the restrained quiet that told Charlie how much he was hurting. 'I know she loves me more than any human being on the planet, even you. I know how much it hurt her not to tell me about coming here, and her title. I know she missed me like hell.' He shook his head. 'But what I don't know is if that will counterbalance her sense of duty and everything this life can offer her. And I don't even know if she sees me as anything but her best friend and big brother. I've tried to tell her how I feel so many times, but if she doesn't want me... I couldn't stand to lose her.' Another sound came from him, like he'd been wounded. 'But now it seems I'll lose her because I've said nothing.'

Charlie shook his head. So many years of painful secrets. He'd been so blind. Blind to Lia's emergence into womanhood; blind to his dearest friend's heart. The blinkers had been ripped away, and he was seeing more than he was ready to know. And the worst part was he had no idea how to help the two people he loved most in the world.

'You'll never lose her altogether, no matter what she decides,' he said, patting Toby's shoulder with awkward male affection. 'She loves you too much.'

'Too much and not enough.' Stark words. 'I couldn't do it, Rip. I've handled it all these years because she needed me, because I was first in her life. But I couldn't stand to be the platonic friend of a princess, knowing she was— Oh, God, if I knew she was in bed with another man...'

A sudden vision filled Charlie's head: the sickening rage he'd felt at the thought of Orakis touching Jazmine, and even his overreaction to Max's innocent comment on Jazmine's beauty. 'So it seems your coming, far from simplifying our impossible decisions, has added extra spice to the pot.'

With clear reluctance and an effort, Toby

grinned. 'I do beg Your Royal Pardon for intruding my emotional turmoil into the heart of your current dilemmas, Rip, my friend.'

Relieved, he slapped Toby on the back. 'That's better. When I can't understand a damn word you say, I know you're back, and the world makes sense again.'

'Again I must beg Your Royal Pardon, Your Bad-Tempered Highness, but I must find Giulia. I understood why she needed to be alone. I know she needed time to assimilate what I said.'

'I bet she did,' Charlie said, his tone dry. 'I'd give her a bit more time with Jazmine. She'll need some girl-time.'

'She does girl-time now?'

At the clear shock on Toby's face, Charlie grinned and nodded. 'The two of them are like sisters; have been from the first day.'

'It seems she's changing, no matter what I do.' Toby's face set hard. 'And—the Grand Duke? What's he to her?'

A sharp knock on the door was followed by a cool voice devoid of humanity. 'Your Highness, your presence is requested in the press-room instantly.'

He mock-sighed as he strode to the door. 'Ain't royal life grand? You don't belong to yourself any more, but to king and country.'

'Keep going, my friend. Tell me it all,' Toby said as Charlie led the way to the press-room. 'The more negatives I know, the more ammunition in my fight.'

'Well, if you want to pile on the kilos, there's the twelve-course dinners, and—' He opened the door and stopped in shock.

The previously always-empty press room was now filled to overflowing with journalists, photographers and staff. Flashes were going off every second, taking shots of a frozen-faced Lia, of a grim Max who stood beside her shielding her from the worst of the attention—and of Jazmine, who stood on the podium trying to answer questions being fired at her every ten seconds.

Jazmine, who for the first time was looking far from the cool-as-ice, touch-me-not princess as she spoke. He could see her shaking.

He began moving through the crowd to her. He had to go to her.

# CHAPTER THIRTEEN

'DOES Hellenia have a new Crown Prince?' someone shouted.

To Charlie's anxious eyes, Jazmine looked small, weary, defenceless, as she spoke, and so *alone* as she faced the constant barrage of questions. Where was the king? 'There has been no decision made by the either the brother or sister as yet—'

Someone else yelled, 'What do you believe his decision will be?'

She didn't move, didn't change expression. 'I have no right to speak for him, on that or any other issue.'

'Do you like him, princess?' a woman yelled over the hubbub.

'Does his Australian upbringing make him un-suitable for the role of future king?' someone else cried almost instantly afterwards.

Her jaw set. 'I have no comment to make on his fitness for the position.'

'But do you like him?' the woman persisted.

Charlie began making his way towards her, elbowing past minders and staff with quiet 'excuse me's' and grim determination.

'Princess Giulia, have you any comment on your decision?'

'When's the wedding, Giulia?'

Lia closed her eyes and shook her head. Being trained thoroughly for this day hadn't prepared her for the sudden, terrifying reality of a press conference. At least Charlie had one advantage, thanks to that fire and the ensuing media circus. He'd been there, done that.

He strode to the platform with all the haughty command his handlers had told him worked from male sovereigns here, and excused himself to Jazmine.

She smiled at him in pure relief. Behind the podium, her hand found his. So cold, so unsure, and she was still here, fighting alone. He wouldn't let her down now.

A quick glance at his sister: there was a final moment to return to obscurity, if she chose. Lia smiled and nodded; her hand moved, a tiny sweep: *do it.* Her strength and courage was back. She was with him. Jazmine was with him.

Time to rise to the occasion, to be worthy of

his wonderful, giving sister and his beautiful, brave princess.

He turned at the podium and said briskly in the Greek Papou had taught them—a relative of the old Koi Greek that was uniquely Hellenican, 'Good morning, ladies and gentlemen of the press. I am Kyriacou Charles Marandis, grandson of the thirteenth Grand Duke of Malascos, son of Athanasius, Marquis of Junoar, and as such the Australian-raised Crown Prince of Hellenia.' He inclined his head as he'd seen the king do to servants and other lesser beings, with the barest hint of a smile. 'I am happy to answer any questions you may have regarding my right to be standing here today.'

As Jazmine gasped and clutched at the hand he held, he repeated the words in English and bowed again.

*Strong and clean, Charlie, combining your birth and breeding with your laid-back Australian accessibility. The press will go wild.*

He was better prepared for the multitude of flashes this time. He stood beside Jazmine, smiling, caressing her cold hand where it couldn't be seen. He allowed the din to die down before he spoke again. 'If you'll pardon me, I'm still not used to so much noise at once. If you could raise your hands…'

All of them rose at once.

'Grey suit, red tie,' Jazmine whispered.

He nodded at that man. 'You, sir.'

'So this means you're definitely taking the position of Crown Prince?'

Charlie inclined his head. 'That's so.' He indicated the next person, after Jazmine had whispered the description.

'Does that mean there will be a royal wedding soon?' the woman asked eagerly.

This was it. Feeling like second-rate goods but unable to show it, he turned to smile down at Jazmine. 'Yes, it does…if she'll have me.'

She covered the microphone for a moment as she looked up at him, her face reflecting the uncertainty. 'Are you sure, Charlie?'

The moment to turn back had come and gone. Now there was only forward. 'I just told the world, didn't I, *loulouthaki*?'

Jazmine's smile was radiant, probably sick with relief that she was free of the worst threat. She must have been feeling like a contestant on the world's worst game-show: *pick Door One—the twice-your-age, twice-married autocrat, Orakis. Pick Door Two: your childhood friend, almost a brother. And Door Three: the crude fireman.*

Well, Door Three it was. 'It seems appropriate

to kiss about now,' he murmured, and at her tiny nod he bent, took her in his arms and kissed her.

He'd never tasted a kiss filled with such relief— and he felt the heady rush that came with knowing he'd done the right thing. He'd saved her.

The press went wild. The flashes were constant for the next minute.

Then the questions resumed, one after the other, blurring into a vague, shadowed memory. He'd never remember what they said, what he said— until a left-field question came from the back corner, a loud, hard bark from a man with a Hellenican accent.

'How do you feel about the allegations that you're unfit to take the throne because of your Italian and Greek commoner's blood, and your total ignorance about the life and ways of our people? How do you feel about your constant failures to do anything right during the past weeks of tutorials?'

Simultaneous gasps filled the room, for which Charlie was grateful. It gave him a few moments to gather his thoughts from every corner of his mind and scramble them back into coherence somehow. To his amazement, he didn't feel the familiar rush of hot-blooded fury. The guy was probably an Orakis supporter, or just doing his job.

The people had the right to know who he was.

As he hesitated Jazmine moved forward, but, with a gentle touch, he stopped her. This had to be his answer.

'As I remember, there have been some comments along these lines for other commoners who became royalty,' he said, with a smile he hoped didn't look forced. 'I had an Italian grandmother, and a Greek mother. I'm not ashamed of it, nor do I think it lessens who I am. My grandmother was a gentle, loving woman who gave up her position amid the Italian nobility to marry my grandfather, and, if my mother was a commoner, she was also—extraordinary. They were the people who defined my life with their kindness, goodness and unselfish giving to others. They made me the person I am, as much as my father or grandfather, and my sister.'

'But that's why the king isn't here today, isn't it?' the man said, his voice deadly cold. 'Can you confirm that the king neither likes nor approves of you as Crown Prince?'

Startled, Charlie answered the first part with truth. 'King Angelis is unwell.'

'My grandfather is confined to a bed at the moment,' Jazmine said quietly into the microphone. 'His doctors are attending to him.'

There followed a few minutes of questions then, on the king's state of health.

Then the man at the back repeated his question, 'Isn't it true, *Prince Kyriacou*, that the king neither likes you nor thinks you worthy of the position you claim as yours?'

'I heard you the first time, sir. I felt the questions on the king's state of health more important to answer first.' He held up a hand as the man began repeating his question. 'Please give me a moment.'

It was obvious to him now what was going on here.

*This was a test.* Orakis had sent this man to try to force him to make a mistake, to become a fool in the eyes of the world.

Why that strengthened him, he had no idea. But the words came to him easily.

'I think we all know that if King Angelis disapproved of me I wouldn't be standing here today—Lord Orakis would. I have tripped over on some of the tests set for me. I don't deny it. But, if I'd failed completely, His Majesty would have put me on the first plane back to Sydney.'

Most heads nodded in agreement. He drew a breath of relief before continuing. Funny how he'd only just seen the truth of what he'd said just now. It did his self-confidence a great deal of good to realize the wily old fox hadn't hated him as much as he'd thought.

'In my view, it's not always people of birth and breeding that have changed the world. Ordinary people have taken key roles, have stepped forward with something to give the world. Some of the world's best-loved people were and are commoners. So, no, I don't think my Italian or Greek blood weakens my position. I hope I have something to give to Hellenia—and I believe the input of my mother and grandmother will help me as future king, to rule with compassion and an understanding of the common people, and to be able to dust myself off and try again when I do fail.' He smiled down at Jazmine, whose face was aglow with pride as she smiled back. 'And, with an extraordinary woman like Princess Jazmine at my side, the failures won't be too often, I'm sure.'

The press went wild again for a few minutes.

'Princess Jazmine!' The same man's deep, harsh voice called over the noise. 'I know for a fact that the man beside you, a common fireman, has failed at the most basic of royal expectations and protocols. No matter what face he puts on it, it's well known that he's been a disappointment to King Angelis from the start. How do you feel about that, since you'll be the one who will have to cover his every mistake?'

Jazmine was leaning into the microphone before the man had finished. She listened to his every word in icy silence. 'Are you finished?'

The man, unintimidated, nodded.

'Then, before all these people, I choose this man for my consort, my husband, whether or not he takes the crown,' she said coolly. Charlie wondered if anyone else heard the unsteady note in her voice as she bared her soul. 'I might have considered Lord Orakis if he had ever saved fifty-four lives or crossed the world to help others, instead of thinking only of his own advantage.'

The murmurs among the press began to swell.

'But that isn't the reason I'm standing here now beside my fiancé.' Her gaze swept the crowd, proud, disdainful, yet still smiling. Regal to her fingertips, his *loulouthaki*, her abundance of passion and fire stoked and slumbering by sheer force of her will. 'I am more committed to my country and my people than ever in their time of need—but this is no morganatic alliance. Common fireman or Crown Prince, I love him for the man he is, not for the compassion and stability he can give my people.'

As she kissed him again, Charlie froze. His

brain switched off the lights and went on holiday without leaving a note. He broke out in a cold sweat, his pulse hammered and his lungs stopped working. And the seconds ticked on. He heard each one—tick, tick—coming closer and closer to the moment Jazmine stopped kissing him and he'd have to answer, and it would be time to face his reckoning.

Because he had absolutely no idea what to say.

Finally she ended the kiss; God knew, he couldn't have, would gladly have kissed her for ever rather than face this moment. Someone yelled, 'Prince Kyriacou, how do you feel about that? Are you in love with the princess?'

*God help me*, was all he could think as he kept staring at Jazmine, watching the radiant certainty fade from her face. Beneath the confident smile and proud eyes she reserved for the press, he saw the dread of knowledge touch her. Why he was here.

*Tick, tick...*

'Charlie?' she whispered, too softly for the press to hear. Her face super-imposed again: the Mona-Lisa princess and the gentle woman who'd bared her soul for his sake, who deserved a true prince and was now stuck with the toad before her.

He coughed and turned to the microphone. 'I beg your pardon. I think my fiancée just melted my brain. The woman's kiss is hotter than any fire I've fought.'

Laughter filled the room. From the side, where his impossible escape-hatch lured him like a siren's call, Toby grinned and gave him a discreet thumbs-up.

But, though she didn't move away, Jazmine's hand released his.

He threw up another frantic prayer, but nothing came. He was on his own. Inane jokes wouldn't help him any more.

A quick glance at Lia showed him she was as scared as him. She knew him too well, knew what was coming.

Toby had his fists in front of him, pumping, up down, up down, in the old fire station signal: get on with it! Get to work!

Nope—still blank. So he settled for truth. It was all he had.

'I'm not a man who talks about private matters in public,' he said quietly. 'Those kinds of words belong to husband and wife alone. I can say, however, that I am deeply committed to the future. I'm committed to my future as Crown Prince, as the heir to the throne—to this nation—and as a husband to my wife. Hellenia needs healing, and my wife-to-be and I are as one in a commitment to helping our country to achieve that aim. And I am completely and totally committed to my bride-to-be. I'm in this for life.'

He knew he ought to kiss Jazmine yet again, but something in her eyes held him off. So he looked around for a moment, testing the reaction to his speech.

He saw Orakis's man slide out of the room, his face dark and thunderous.

He saw Toby grin and nod.

Lia's gaze was trained on Jazmine, with that secret 'girl's together' look on her face.

Not knowing what else to do, he kissed Jazmine's cold, unresponsive lips for a fourth time, and the flashes popped and the cheers were spontaneous.

It seemed there were only two people he hadn't fooled: the two women who meant the most to him.

He'd screwed it up again. He'd given all he could, yet he'd failed Jazmine. Again.

# CHAPTER FOURTEEN

FINALLY she was alone.

In the suite that wasn't hers, in a place that had never felt like home, Jazmine kicked off the four-inch heels she'd been told gave her dignity and sat on the bed. It seemed a pathetic kind of borrowed dignity, a disguise, a mask of pretence, being someone she wasn't.

She had no dignity left; she had no pretence to hide behind, no pride. And the worst part was she couldn't blame anyone but herself. She'd risked it all, she'd bared her soul to the world, showed her heart for all to see, and he'd been *kind*.

Fourteen minutes. It was all she had before she had to face him again, and she had nothing. No story to tell, no lie to cover it over. She could try to laugh it off, use Orakis as an excuse—whatever rids us of his threat, right?—but she'd stripped off her mask for good. He knew the truth—and he'd been kind…

If she'd eaten anything at all in the past eight
hours, she'd have wanted to throw up. She
wished she could. Her stomach seemed to be
churning on air.

She couldn't do it, couldn't face him, not when
he was making a sacrifice for her and she couldn't
say no, couldn't stop him. She'd rather he'd lost
it and yelled at her than pitied her.

The door burst open without warning, and he
stood there in the entry, chest heaving, his eyes
black with fury. 'Get away from here' was all he
said.

The security detail behind him backed off to a
discreet distance.

Jazmine sat on the bed, too tired to move, and
watched him slam the door shut and stride to her,
his face like a thunderclap about to burst open and
pour over her.

The firecracker was back, she noted with an
odd relief. Explosions she knew, she could cope
with. Not *kindness*. She waited for him to start.

'I can't apologize for what I said, Jazmine. I
was honest with you.'

She blinked. His face was dark with fury; why
was he speaking so quietly, with such strange
control? 'All right.' She couldn't think of anything
else to say.

'I have enough changes to cope with. I'm learning protocol, politics, religion, how to walk, talk, bow and smile, and the titles and history of noble families around the world. Next week I start learning to fly planes and jumping out of choppers into the ocean, for crying out loud. I have to learn in a few months what you learned in a lifetime. If I'm going to become the kind of prince Hellenia needs, I can't deal with *feelings*, too.'

He seemed to wait for her to say something. 'I see.'

Her compliance seemed to confuse him; he began pacing, as if she'd argued. 'Toby's coming has only made more mess, but he's my brother, and he's in pain. He'd be there for me, the way he was for Lia. He stood by us after everything eleven years ago.'

'Of course,' she said, feeling oddly numb and stupid.

The glance became a narrow-eyed assessment. 'I saved you from Orakis. I agreed to be your prince. What more do you want from me?'

Light dawned on her. He'd given her everything he had, and he felt guilty he couldn't give more? 'Nothing,' she said softly.

He went on as if he hadn't heard. 'I swear I'll be faithful, Jazmine. I'll be the best husband I know how.'

He waited again. Her cue. 'I know you will.'

'I don't know how to be a prince or a king, but my father and grandfather were excellent husbands. I can do it.'

How could she want to smile when she hurt so much? 'I believe you.'

'But that's all I've got.' His eyes burned into hers now. 'Do you understand? I'll be your prince. I'll do my best to be king when the time comes. I'll be a faithful and honest husband. I'll be a good father to our kids. But that's all, Jazmine.'

Her cue again. 'I understand.'

And she did. He wanted her to back off, to give him space. Two weeks after coming here, he had truly done all she'd expected of him in the beginning, and he'd brought heart, thought and kindness to the role. He was already a prince, without the coronation; he was committed to Hellenia. He'd brought passion and laughter to her life, and had shared more of his secret self than she'd dreamed in the beginning.

She was being unfair in expecting more.

'It's all right, Charlie,' she said softly. 'I do understand—and thank you. Thank you for saving me, for saving Hellenia, and for salvaging my pride today.'

He shifted back, looking as if she'd impaled

him instead of letting him off the hook. 'I do like you, okay? But I don't—'

'I said, it's all right.' She spoke over him before he could say the rest. Unable to bear hearing what she already knew. 'You don't have to explain any more. I understand. Princess and prince, queen and king, wife and husband; they're our roles. And parents, when the time comes. I'm a princess; controlling my emotions was drilled into me from birth. You won't have any tragic scenes to endure. We'll be excellent friends who happen to be married.' She lifted her chin and smiled at him. 'Now, if you'll excuse me, it's time for dinner. I need to change.'

She padded to the dressing room without looking back. If she did, he'd see how she'd repaid his honesty with lies. For his sake.

*Six weeks later*

'That was a productive day.' Jazmine sighed, closed her eyes and rested against the leather seating of the car as they left the third village at the day. She'd always refused to take limousines to the ravaged villages—she'd said it was like rubbing the differences between them in their faces. But the king insisted on their taking security cars with bullet-proof glass. Charlie called them their 'Pope mobiles'.

'Yeah—yes,' Charlie replied, watching her with a hunger he could barely rein in. It had been two days since he'd last kissed her.

'The apprenticeship scheme seems to be taking off everywhere we've instigated it.' She tugged at the shirt she wore; it was touched with perspiration.

'Yes, it has.' His gaze roamed her lovely form, damp and gently lush.

'I think we'll be able to initiate the scheme in another six villages within a few months. Wealth certainly seems to be begetting prosperity.' She smiled lazily. 'Your first decision for the crown and country was inspired. And your second really made the people love you—importing retired firefighters from Australia under Toby's direction, teaching the volunteers via interpreters. The Malascos fortune is certainly being put to good use, building fire stations, preventing fire and repairing damage.'

Did he say, 'Uh-huh?' He had no idea; he was lost in watching her lips move.

'The press and the people are lapping it up. They already adore you and Lia both, thanks to her ideas to help widows, orphans and divorced women. The flood of disaffected youth heading to Orakis's army has stopped and come back to us, because you're saving their villages and bringing in good changes, while preserving their way of life. You'll soon be a legend, you know. Statues and parks in your name.'

'Thanks,' he croaked, his desire fast reaching physical agony. He felt like a pervert of the worst kind.

It was always the same when they were alone together. He wanted and ached and burned…and always had to make the first move. It was becoming embarrassing—downright humiliating, actually—as if he was lusting after his best friend.

Not that she ever repulsed him. She welcomed his touch with a smile, and gave kiss for kiss. She just didn't *look* at him that way any more. She didn't say Char-r-liee, with that husky, blurry voice that drove him over the edge, or wind her fingers through his hair, or come to his room for late-night talks or walks through secret passages—or to hold him until he slept. No radiant smiles. No shimmering eyes as she smiled at him. She'd become exactly what she'd promised—an excellent friend and helpmate.

She was there, and yet she wasn't. It was driving him demented.

During the past six weeks Jazmine had kept her word as perfectly as she did everything else. No scenes; no tears or demands to endure. She was there beside him as she'd always been, teaching, guiding, encouraging him. She showed the way to lead her country by just being Jazmine. She smiled at him, she talked to him.

When he touched her, when he kissed her, she never rejected him or made excuses. The sweet fire he loved was in her response, if not quite the same. Something was missing; he just couldn't define what. But at least he had no need to worry she'd be a sulky wife who'd blackmail him before he could gain access to her bed.

Charlie was relieved about it. Of course he was. She was strong, she was a survivor, and it wasn't as if he was anything special; he was just another guy.

Okay, so she couldn't move on with him in her life, but she'd survived far worse. She'd shown her strength constantly during the past six weeks— when they'd been through the coronation and the engagement party, a zillion wedding shoots and interviews—and she'd been radiant and smiling through each one. And the moment their audiences had disappeared the loving fiancée had become the friend, keeping her distance unless the screaming need to touch her overwhelmed him. And when the kisses ended she walked away with a smile. No demands, no tears.

She didn't seem to be pining for what he couldn't give her. She had the palace, the prince, the crown, and the kids yet to come. She had a magnificent wedding gown, and a ring they'd chosen together from samples sent by the best jewellers in Europe. She seemed contented enough.

So why did he feel so bad?

And why did he miss her so much, when she was right there with him?

Her voice drifted into his tortured thoughts with the soft huskiness of sleep; the same huskiness she used to have when she wanted him. 'So tomorrow, when the—'

'Not now,' he growled, put up the shield so the driver couldn't see, and dragged her against him.

She smiled, her eyes pleasant—half-empty, half-full; half-*something*—and lifted her face for his kiss.

*Passive.*

He pushed an errant curl from her face with some kind of fever. 'Kiss *me* this time, *loulouthaki*.' His voice was guttural with need, calling her by her nickname for the first time in weeks. Trying to push her—into what, he didn't know.

Her smile changed, became bittersweet, touched, tanged with loss, but she kissed him. She kissed him as an old friend would on seeing him again, and he couldn't handle it. Furious at her for being so obedient when she never had been before, he moulded her against him. 'No, *loulouthaki*—*kiss me*. Kiss me like you used to.'

She did as he asked, kissing him with her lips soft and parted and her ready passion coming to life; but still the gentle shell surrounding her didn't break. Even in the middle of a kiss that fried his brain, he felt her reserve enveloping her, impenetrable. Giving of her body, but protecting her heart. Keeping her real self in hiding.

Passion without feelings. Wanting him without caring.

God help him, it was everything he'd asked from her. It was the meaningless kind of relationship he was used to with women.

Except this was Jazmine. The woman who saw right through to his heart, and gave him what he asked for without taking in return. The woman with whom he would exchange vows before God and his people in a few weeks was treating him like a friend when he wanted a friend, and acted as a good-time guy when all he wanted to do was touch her. Easy, uncomplicated, fun.

But this was Jazmine, who was anything but those things. His honest Jazmine was living a lie, and he was making her do it.

What fool had said, 'you can't always get what you want'? He had it now, in his arms and his life, and right now he'd exchange the lot of it for an hour—a *minute*—of the fascinating, frustrating, adorable Jazmine he'd had at the beginning. With her emotional withdrawal, the sunshine and laughter had gone missing. No warmth or caring, no holding him, no sweetness and light, no addictive whispers of his name…no lifting onto tiptoes to kiss him, no innocent hands exploring him with ardent eagerness.

He was fast learning the truth of the saying, 'be careful what you wish for'.

God forgive him for his stupidity, he had it all right.

He hated himself for pushing her into becoming someone who smiled and kissed him on cue because she needed him to stay but no longer wanted it, no longer wanted *him*. He ended the kiss that disgusted him, because he couldn't stop trying to make her be what she'd been before becoming this obedient robot. 'It's all right,' he said dully. 'Go to sleep.'

She frowned as she moved back to her corner, her gaze searching his with hidden anxiety— the look he called the 'door one' option, if he left. 'Charlie—'

'No, don't,' he said roughly. 'It's not your fault, and you know it. I'm not going anywhere, Jazmine; I wouldn't leave you to Orakis, so stop being so compliant!'

As if he'd waved a magic wand over her, the fear vanished. She sat back against the seat, her head tilted in an intelligent, enquiring look. 'You're not happy.'

'Would you be?' he snapped.

A brow lifted as her head tilted more, searching out secrets he couldn't recognize. 'So what's wrong?'

Goaded by her calmness, he grabbed her by the shoulders. 'You tell me. It's like you've gone away and only your body's here.'

She lifted her hands in that elegant shrug of hers. 'Isn't that what you asked for?'

'Yeah, well, I don't like it,' he muttered, knowing he was being a hypocrite, but he didn't care.

Slowly, she nodded, her mouth slightly pursed. 'If you don't want me like this, what is it you *do* want from me, Charlie?'

How could he say it, after pushing her into becoming this? 'What do you think I want?'

Suddenly her chin lifted, her eyes sparked with life and fire, and the emotionless, compliant Jazmine slipped from her like an unwanted skin.

The real woman sat beside him, complex, fascinating and adorable, all in an instant: the Jazmine he couldn't resist. 'Is this what you want—the woman I was before?'

He'd dragged her back to him before she finished speaking, his mouth on hers, and she moaned and thrust her hands into his hair, exploring him with a hunger to match his. She pulled him down on top of her, thrusting her hips against his. Taking charge with touch and kiss, using lips and tongue and soft, shuddering breaths to sensual advantage. Moaning and whispering tiny gasps: his name, just his name. *'Char-r-liee...'*

*'Loulouthaki mou.* Ah, yeah, ah... I've missed you so bad,' he mumbled between kisses. 'The real you. Stay with me. Just the way you are.'

She held him off, looking into his eyes. 'The trouble with this woman is she doesn't turn on and off on demand. This woman, the woman you want, has needs, has demands of her own.'

'Thank God for it.' He kissed her throat and felt her shiver. Yes, that was it. Ah, so good to have her back where she belonged...

She trailed her fingers down his neck and back, and he groaned. 'Sorry, Charlie,' the soft, relentless voice continued—and she pushed him off her. 'This woman comes complete with the things you demanded I leave out of our relationship.'

How could she be all rosy and warm with passion, so beautiful and alive, yet so cool and clear-headed at the same time? His head was spinning, and his body still pounded with the painful 'got to have her now' feeling she could inspire in him with a touch.

'This woman lives and breathes and wants and aches, Charlie.' The softest kiss on his neck made him groan out loud, dying for more. 'I laugh and cry. Sometimes I yell.' Tender, clinging kisses, once, twice on his aching mouth. 'And I *hurt*, too. You don't want the guilt that goes with that, remember?'

Only half the words went into his muddled brain and stayed. He was still locked into what he'd been aching to have for weeks, and he couldn't believe she was doing this to him now! It was like she was Salome, dancing before him, slowly stripping off the veils of pliancy covering the woman he wanted, needed, had to have, while his head was on a plate. At this moment he was almost willing to give anything to have her.

Damn women and their multi-tasking.

'And the trouble is, Charlie, that's me. This is who I am, and my feelings are part of the deal. If you push that part of me away, you push all of me away.'

Suddenly his brain came back to clarity and focus—fear had a way of doing that to a man. He stilled, and stared down at her. 'So we're back to that.'

She met his gaze, fearless and honest. 'This is by your choice, Charlie. You're the one who wants the real woman.'

He moved to his side of the car, putting space between them. He had to think with his brain, not the parts of him screaming, 'do it, do anything to have her…' 'You're trapping me.' He heard the bitterness in his voice.

'And you think that's unfair? You think you're the only one? *You* took on the job. *You* made the choice. Nobody forced you.'

That wasn't true. Circumstances—Orakis—had forced his hand; even Jazmine had, by being who she was. But none of it was her fault. She'd done her best to give him freedom to choose. But because she was who she was, her own courageous, wonderful self, she'd forced him—forced him to *want* to live up to her standard, to be a better man.

But how could he say it? It probably made no sense to anyone but him.

'If it makes you feel better, you've trapped me too. You have from the start,' she said, her voice flat. 'You rode into my palace, the brave fireman into the burning building, and, no matter how many times I warned you, you kept saving me.' Her defiant gaze held pride and unashamed pain. 'Even telling me your secrets was for me, wasn't it? You had to save me from you, but you never thought of the consequences.' She sighed and fiddled with the cup holder built into the car door. 'That's your problem, Charlie. You like to save people on a one-time-only basis, to go home to your quiet, safe world alone, because you don't want to feel. And you don't want others to feel. Well, life isn't black and white. You can't tailor the world to your wants or needs. Like the rest of us, you have to live in a real world where people do make mistakes—all of us—and we do get hurt. You became my hero once too often, and I'm in love with you.'

Strange that she could say 'I love you' with such quiet loathing, as if she hated him. Even stranger that he was hurting too, and feeling, and wishing...

Finally she let his gaze go, and he almost gasped with relief; he'd felt like a pinned butterfly, a specimen she was tearing apart piece by piece. When she released him, he tried to snap back to the person he'd always been, but something had changed and he didn't know what.

'So take the woman with feelings, or without.' She turned her head, looking out her side of the car window. 'Make your choice and live with it, Charlie. I have to.'

His head was banging every which way now. She could do this to him, turn him inside out, make him feel heaven and hell at once, make him live.

And leave him with utterly no idea what to say until he blurted out things he didn't know he was thinking or feeling until he said them. She dragged truth from him because she made him feel like the world's worst coward. He could rescue kids from burning buildings, but he couldn't allow himself to care. He knew how to risk his life, but didn't know how to take chances with his heart.

As the car passed the gates of the summer palace, he knew he had to say something or she'd know him for the pathetic, terrified man he was, a man who could take on a country but couldn't handle one five-foot-three woman he—he *what*…?

'I think—I think I love you.'

And he gasped. Had he really said that? And how could he feel so liberated, when his throat had closed up and his heart had become twice its normal size, suffocating him? He was going to die, to die.

He had his last, panicked thought: *at least she'll be happy now. She won. I loved her for all of a minute.*

The shocking sting of her palm hitting his cheek snapped his body back to its normal pace and rhythm. Thank God; she'd seen his panic attack and had saved his life.

Then he gasped again. He'd be willing to bet she'd never called any man *that* word before.

'How could you, Charlie? *How could you?*' she cried, her face pale and her eyes dark with devastation. She scrambled out of the car with utterly no grace, and bolted for the doors.

And he knocked his head against the luxurious leather seating, over and over.

What had he done this time? What had he said or done that was so wrong?

# CHAPTER FIFTEEN

*Four days later*
*The forty-fifth anniversary of King Angelis's reign*

CHARLIE and Toby sat on their favourite stools at the bar in a quiet corner of the summer palace's ballroom. Charlie had circulated the room, spoken to dignitaries and assisted the elderly. Now he was enjoying a quiet beer with Toby, waiting for the call to dinner.

Five hundred noble guests from around the world had come to celebrate this milestone—and, given the king's increasingly frail state of health, it seemed it would be the last.

Charlie's gaze tracked Jazmine's graceful progress around the room. She ought to be here laughing with him, relaxing at this special party, not having to deal with the guy from the *Hellenican Observer*. Didn't the guy know her grandfather's health was more than a political issue to her? Couldn't the man see the sheen in her eyes, the sadness in her smile? It was visible to him even from this distance. It was all he could do to keep sitting there. If he thought she'd welcome him…

'Why doesn't this place have a pool table?' he snapped for no good reason.

'Two or three pool tables, and a few dartboards,' Toby agreed in a growl. Max had just joined Lia, who was surrounded by a group of international admirers.

Charlie picked up his beer and swilled it down with no appreciation for its import costs, imagining Jazmine lying beside him with that slow, sleepy smile that made him forget titles and duty and everything but her.

Jazmine had extricated herself from the journalist and had stationed herself beside the king, who was having difficulty speaking to his guests. He would be returning to his bed as soon as dinner was over.

Charlie half-lifted from the stool, ready to help. Jazmine caught his eye and looked away, making the crowd around her grandfather laugh at something she said. She didn't want or need him; she was coping alone. She didn't want him.

'Why is it I can run a bloody country, I can make

eight million people happy, and I can't tell a woman I love her without her hitting me?' he muttered.

Jazmine had been immersed in the final details of this celebration dinner since she'd slapped him. Since it was all prearranged, he couldn't accuse her of avoiding him, but she'd had no time to hear him or sort things out. All he wanted was for things to be as they'd been between them—but, like everything else in his life, he'd woken up too late.

Toby shrugged, his gaze riveted on Lia, whose arm had slipped through Max's as they shared a smile about something. 'It's the way God made us. We're the bigger and stronger, we can build things and fight fires, but women run circles around us in emotions or argument. They crush us to dust every time. We never win.' Toby downed his beer.

Charlie tried for a third time to catch Jazmine's eye, but she turned obliquely so she was at a ninety-degree angle from him. Her unspoken 'don't touch me, don't come near me' was so loud she might as well have screamed it across the room.

'What did I do that was so wrong?' Charlie demanded, thudding his glass down so hard the beer sloshed over onto the beautiful polished mahogany, and some dignitary or other who'd been approaching him scuttled away. 'I *told* her, Grizz. Wasn't that what she wanted?'

Toby shrugged again. 'Don't ask me. I don't have a clue... obviously.'

Charlie shook the beer off his hand, but grabbed the washcloth from the bartender when he started to clean the mess. 'My mess. My job.' He wiped down the counter, and handed it back. 'Sorry,' he said gruffly.

Slowly, the bartender smiled. 'It's fine, Your Highness. And, if I may say so, I think you're doing Hellenia, and the royal family a great deal of good.'

Charlie frowned, arrested by the words for no reason he could fathom. 'Why?'

The older man smiled. 'Change at this time in Hellenia's history is good, sir. After the war and suffering, you've come in and done the things we believe Princess Jazmine would do if she was a man. They like having a man of action in the palace.'

*If she was a man...* The words ping-ponged around in his brain. There was something there— something significant, profound.

During dinner, he watched Jazmine take care of the frail king without taking away the old man's dignity. He watched her direct the staff when they came to her with questions. He watched her discreetly listening to the conversation around her and join in when appropriate, murmuring to her grandfather when his voice was needed.

Lia walked round her chair to Jazmine's and said something. Jazmine murmured to a member of staff, who spoke to someone else, who delivered no more wine to a bordering-on-belligerent dignitary who'd had a bit much to drink. Lia and Jazmine worked together beautifully, seamlessly, to ensure the night's success—but it was Jazmine who directed it all, Jazmine whom everyone trusted to get it right.

Everyone trusted Jazmine every time—the king, the diplomatic staff, servants, the people, the media. She did everything in the best interests of others.

*If she was a man.*

That was it. That was it!

*The next day*

The press-room was filled to overflowing again for the new Crown Prince's first self-called press conference.

Cameras began rolling from every TV station or affiliate in Europe the moment Charlie walked in from the huge corner-door. Flashes popped. Security men flanked him and stood in every row, armed and dangerous. Every member of the press had been searched for weapons.

But, because no one had a clue why Charlie had called the conference, they waited for him to start.

She wasn't here. He'd asked her to come, but she'd claimed royal duties.

It didn't matter. He knew her well enough to be sure that she'd come once she knew what he intended. Lia would be right behind her.

Once again, he strode to the podium with the regal bearing he'd been taught. Once again, he gave the flawless introduction.

And then he got to the point.

'Ladies and gentlemen of Hellenia, and the press—I am a modern man, as you all know. My Hellenican family was traditional enough to believe a man is the head of the house. But my father and grandfather taught me deep respect for women and their right to have a place in the world—and a say in their future. My past career as a firefighter, and my immersion into Australian culture, only reinforced that belief.

'I fought fires the same way I intend to fight for what is best for this, my new country. Hellenia is a beautiful country, with people who want a life that blends the best of their ancient traditions with modern life. She has her own statutes and laws, as do all nations. I fully intend to uphold those traditions when they are best for my people.

'King Angelis has been a magnificent monarch during these uncertain times. But for every nation there comes time to change—and I believe it's time to make a change.'

He looked around the room. He could probably have heard a pin drop. They were waiting for the announcement.

He glanced to the right, to the door reserved for royalty's entrance. Toby, stationed by the door, shrugged. Jazmine still wasn't here.

So he went on with the speech he'd stayed up all night to write.

'During my last press conference, one of you made a very good point. I'm new to this country. I come from common stock as well as noble. I grew up completely ignorant of this nation. And, though I'm doing my best to rectify this ignorance, it's clear that I *will* make mistakes, will judge the people by the standards in which I was raised, by the only life I've known until now. I also know that many of my people are relying on the excellent guidance I have behind me to do what's best for Hellenia, to be the best king I can be.

'However, I am not so certain this is the right way. I *am* a stranger. I *am* ignorant. It's only by accident of birth that I'm here now—a fact of which I'm very well aware. If the laws didn't state that a male must take the throne unless there are no male-line descendants left, I wouldn't be standing here—likely, I'd be standing at a pub in Sydney.' He grinned, let them laugh, and added, 'Princess Jazmine would be standing here instead, as the person with the greatest right to rule this country.'

The murmurs began; they whispered questions among themselves.

He cleared his throat of the nerves filling it, and continued. 'When I thought of that, I realized that she ought to be here now, today, as your future ruler. Princess Jazmine has devoted her life to this country and its people. She is a strong, intelligent and courageous woman who has put her own safety on the line time after time to help her people. If the laws were different, you would have the ruler you deserve.'

He paused to let that sink in.

'This is the change I will propose at the next meeting of the king and ministers: this five-hundred-year-old law needs to be revoked. The most direct descendant of the last ruler, be they male or female, should take the throne. I propose that when our strong and excellent King Angelis passes away, or decides to abdicate, Hellenia should enjoy the rule of the best person they could have on the throne: Princess Jazmine.'

The room erupted into a cacophony of light and sound: strobe-flashing and yelled questions.

'So does this mean you're stepping down as Crown Prince, Your Highness?'

'Are you returning to Australia?'

'Did you and the princess break up?'

Charlie allowed the questions to keep coming thick and fast as he summoned his thoughts, ready to answer each question with all the patience he could muster. Willing himself with all the self-control at his command not to keep looking at the door. Looking for Jazmine couldn't help now. She was already filling his head too much.

*Come to me*, loulouthaki. *Tell me that, for once, I got it right. Give me that shimmering look and tell me you've forgiven me for being so slow and stupid, not knowing how much I love you. Kiss me and tell me you still love me.*

But even if she didn't come, if she couldn't forgive him, he knew in his heart and soul that he'd done the right thing, both for Hellenia and the woman he loved.

He was still amazed he hadn't thought of it within days of arriving here. He'd known he was the wrong person for the job, and Jazmine was utterly right to rule; but he hadn't seen until last night that, if he had the power to take the title or walk away, he had the power to propose change.

But he needed to effect change. And that was why he'd called a press conference first, instead of using the privacy of a session of the lords who pretended to help the king run the country.

If the people were behind him in this, the press would know.

A small commotion to his right made him want to smile. She was here.

Moments later an exquisitely dressed Jazmine was beside him on the podium, her lovely face filled with a confusion and fury she couldn't even hide for the cameras. Without even looking at the assembled press, she dragged him to the absolute back of the room, away from microphones but not from speculation. '*What* do you think you're doing, you idiot?'

Relief flooded him. He could handle anything, even her abuse, if she was talking to him. If she was here with him, he could do anything. 'Ah, so it only takes giving up a kingdom to make you take the time to talk to me? You set your asking price too low, princess,' he said softly, smiling down at her.

She looked shaken. 'You called a press conference and gave up your position to make me *talk
to you*?' she whispered incredulously.

'Well, that, and one small fact: you're the best
person for the job. I don't know why I didn't see
it before.' He kept smiling. He probably looked
like a dork, but he didn't care. He'd missed her
so badly and she was here.

'You're an *idiot*,' she repeated for his ears alone.
'You've made such a mess and now I have to fix it!'

His brows lifted. 'A mess, princess? Look out
there.' He waved a hand to the rest of the room.

Taken aback by his confidence, she
turned...and saw the standing ovation, heard the
calls of her name.

She blinked. 'It—it can't happen, Charlie. The
ruler must be male.'

Loving her sweet confusion, wanting to believe
but not daring, he took her hand in his and smiled
for the barrage of cameras. 'Smile and agree, and
bide your time,' he whispered in her ear, quoting
her words back to him. 'This is the time, Jazmine.
If we wait until the king dies, I'm automatically
king—and then it's too late.'

She turned to him, her face stricken. 'You're
leaving?'

The roars for attention from the press grew

louder. It wasn't time for personal declarations, unless he combined the best of both.

He drew her forward to the microphone. 'Ladies and gentlemen of the press, I give you the person I believe will be the best future ruler you could have—my future wife, the woman I love, Jazmine Marandis.' Knowing now the power of the press could be turned his way, he thought of kneeling but rejected it as too dramatic, so he turned her around to him, took both hands in his, and looked deeply in her eyes. Speaking too low for the microphone, he murmured, 'That is, if you still want to marry me after I threw a surprise of this magnitude into your lap.'

Slowly, she looked down and back up. Her hands trembled. 'Charlie...'

'I didn't do this to prove I love you, *loulou-thaki*,' he whispered. 'I believe you were born for this. I believe I finally got something right here. Nothing ever felt so right before. I believe this is right for Hellenia, not just right for you. And I'll be at your side whenever you need me. I'm not going anywhere—for the rest of our lives.'

Her eyes shimmered as her smile slowly came to life. 'I'll always need you.'

He'd never wanted to kiss her more than now. But she'd already turned to the press, who'd been following the quiet drama with avid interest. 'Ladies and gentlemen of the press, please be seated.'

Her tone brooked no denial, no argument or question. She had something to say.

'I can honestly say Prince Kyriacou didn't shock *you* alone. I knew he'd called a conference, but had no inkling of his intention until I heard his announcement. That's obvious, I suppose, by my reaction.' She smiled and did the hand-shrug thing he loved, and everyone laughed. 'Unfortunately, as much as his gesture touches me, I believe Hellenia isn't ready just yet for change of such magnitude.'

Charlie's heart hit his gut. No, no, he couldn't be wrong this time! Not when it felt so right. She couldn't do this. But he had to trust her now. If he took over, it would look as though he didn't think she could handle the job already.

When the hubbub died down, Jazmine spoke again. 'I do believe Prince Kyriacou has it right; it's time for change.' Smiling, she turned and reached for his hand. He came forward at her tugging. 'I believe that, with the blessing of my grandfather and the House of Hereditary Lords, the next rulership could become a joint one. A co-rulership would bring the energy, fresh direction and knowledge of the common people that is

Prince Kyriacou's greatest strength, and my knowledge of Hellenican people and history.'

This time the room didn't erupt, it exploded, as the press surged to their feet, cheering and asking questions.

And Charlie, stunned yet not surprised, looked at her. 'I should have known you'd one-up me, princess. You get it right every time.'

She smiled up at him. 'Only when my wonderful prince gives me the incredible, new and fresh ideas I can find ways to improve on. I'd never have thought of this on my own, Charlie. And I'd never have thought of going public with it, to strengthen our position with the people's approval.' The eyes he loved so much shimmered—not with tears, but with love. 'We're going to make such a wonderful team, *eros mou.*'

*My love.*

And she turned back to the press, answering questions as if she hadn't just made all his dreams come true.

But then, that was the woman he loved: his courageous, strong little flower.

After ten interminable minutes of answering questions, his hand caressed hers behind the cover of the podium with the Hellenican crest. 'How soon can we get out of here? I've got to kiss you soon. I've got to touch you, *loulouthaki*, or I'll hit something,' he growled in her ear.

A small smile curved her mouth. Her eyes danced. 'Such is the life of royalty. You have to learn to wait, from bathroom visits to making love,' she whispered back...but her thumb moved from its linked position and softly stroked his palm. 'But I promise I'll make it worth the wait.'

His heart and body went into fast meltdown. 'Something tells me you'll always make the wait worthwhile.'

They smiled at each other, warm, tender, intimate—and, too late, they both realized they'd totally missed the most recent question.

# EPILOGUE

'AND now, I'd like to ask the bride and groom to take the floor for the traditional bridal waltz. Prince Kyriacou personally chose the song, and wishes to dedicate it to his bride.' Toby, in his combined role of best man and master of ceremonies, smiled and made a sweeping motion with his hand.

Charlie got to his feet, and, keeping Jazmine's hand in his, kissed it softly as he led her to the perfectly polished floor of the state ballroom. 'Mine at last,' he murmured in her ear.

Jazmine's heart skipped a beat at the look in his eyes, at his touch. In the past few weeks, they'd come so close to making love, over and over—but, no matter how many times she'd begged him, no matter how many times she got him close to nakedness and madness, he'd refused to cross the line.

'You deserve the perfect prince and courtship, *loulouthaki*. But, since you're stuck with me, you'll at least get this much: the most perfect wedding night I can give you,' he'd tell her every time. 'Not much longer to wait.'

Tonight was finally the night.

Once on the floor, Charlie didn't sweep her into the dance they'd been practising for weeks. The orchestra stumbled to a halt as he knelt at her feet—and, startled, she watched him gently lift one throbbing foot and remove the four-inch heel from it.

Then he did the same for the other foot. He winked at her and tossed them over to Toby, who caught them with the air of a plan fulfilled.

'But Charlie—'

'The cameras are gone now.' That had been the deal—their reception was theirs alone after weeks of giving of themselves to the people and press. Their honeymoon, on the traditional Aegean island owned by the ruling family, would be totally private and completely protected.

She nibbled at her inside lip. Oh, he knew her too well—he knew her love-hate relationship with heels, and she'd been standing for hours for the photo shoots. Even though they'd since had dinner, her feet still throbbed. 'But everyone else...'

He grinned at her. 'What, you can turn history on its ear by becoming the first co-ruling queen, but you can't shock a few old stick-in-the-muds at our wedding?'

She had to laugh. It was true—the coronation date was set for six weeks' time.

Grandfather had told them both a week ago that he was ready to abdicate, due to failing health. He'd kissed Jazmine's cheek, and said with the approval of the people and House of Hereditary Lords the five-hundred-year-old law of succession would change. She'd proven herself worthy to be co-ruling queen. And Charlie, he said, was ready to be a king in the best mixture of modern ideas and respect for tradition. Charlie had almost fallen off his seat, hearing Grandfather calling him by his preferred name.

Approval for them both at last—and Jazmine would treasure the words for ever. She was going to be queen, with the king she adored at her side. Her laughing, heroic, unconventional Charlie, who thought it appropriate for a princess to go barefoot at her own wedding.

As if walking into her thoughts, he winked again. 'You know you want to.'

She bit her lip, but the grin peeped out. 'I hate you sometimes, you know that?'

He brushed his cheek against hers. 'We belong to the world, but today it's just us, Jazmine. Our wedding, our dance. Just you and me.' He smiled into her eyes, and she melted, as she always did for him.

He lifted her onto his shod feet. 'I won't make any mistakes if I have you right here.' Gently, he kissed her.

The orchestra struck up the song again—and they danced an inch or two closer than protocol demanded, and just a beat slower than they ought. And she loved every romantic moment of it. Even when the floor became crowded with guests, she couldn't see them. All she felt was Charlie. All she wanted, all she needed, was right here in her arms.

Then the song the orchestra played sank into her consciousness, and Toby's words: *Unforgettable.* 'Oh.' Tears rushed to her eyes. 'Oh, Charlie…'

'If you weren't unforgettable, I'd have disappeared long ago.' He smiled and touched his forehead to hers. 'As much as I'd like to believe I stayed, that I took on the job, for all the right reasons—the people, my heroic nobility—the simple truth is, I couldn't leave. I couldn't leave *you.*'

'You're making me cry,' she whispered.

But the tears had been there from the moment she'd awoken this morning.

The room filled with roses had been traditional

and expected; but the funny card he'd sent with them—hand-drawn, with a small, white flower sticking stubbornly to a weed wearing a crown—was so uniquely Charlie, she'd felt she'd burst with love. The inside had held only five words: thank you for being you.

She'd cherish the card all her life.

Then he'd replaced her bridal bouquet of white roses and hothouse flowers. The flowers he'd sent her were unfamiliar, like small, white stars.

'His Highness had them imported from Austria,' Charlie's new personal assistant had told her when he'd delivered them.

Jazmine frowned. 'Don't you mean Australia?'

He'd shaken his head and smiled. 'Edelweiss is an Austrian flower, Your Highness. Prince Kyriacou asked that you read the card.'

Confused, wondering why he'd send these instead of an Australian flower which might mean something to him, she'd opened the envelope.

He'd drawn some musical notes, a rough map of Hellenia, and had written one line: *bless my homeland for ever.*

Her maid and Lia, maid of honour, had had to reapply her make-up after that.

She'd walked down the aisle to him on Grandfather's arm—he'd practised walking, using a cane, right up until today. And, though Charlie hadn't seemed to take his eyes from her, when Grandfather had faltered he'd nodded. Max had quietly come up behind the ailing king, and, without touching him or lessening his pride, had let Grandfather know he was there.

And then, during the traditional wedding, he'd asked to say something. The priest seemed to have expected it, and nodded.

Charlie had turned to Grandfather, and bowed with the deepest respect. Jazmine had seen Grandfather's eyes mist up, and he smiled.

Then Charlie had said, 'People have called me a hero, in the past and now. But in history the real heroes have risen because of one thing, and fallen by it also: the strength of home and love, and the kind of faith only the right woman can give. I had none of those, Jazmine, until you. So from my heart, my princess bride, I thank you for choosing me. I thank you for making me the man I've always wanted to become.'

It was a good thing Lia had brought spare make-up for the photo shoots...

'Uh-oh. Look at that.'

Startled from her thoughts by Charlie's murmur in her ear, she looked to where he indicated. 'Oh, dear.'

The best man and maid of honour were dancing as tradition dictated, but, like Charlie and Jazmine, Toby and Lia were an inch or two closer than necessary…and swaying into each other. Toby dipped Lia with consummate grace—apparently he'd done ballroom lessons with Lia years before—but brought her back to his lips. And despite the public scrutiny Lia swayed into Toby with a dreaming look on her face, closed her eyes and kissed him.

Charlie sighed. 'We're going to have to do something about that.'

'After coronation,' she agreed.

'After our honeymoon,' he corrected, his eyes filled with meaning. 'We need it sorted—but not until then.' He gave a low growl as he saw Max heading towards them. 'Max is coming. More royal waiting-time before I can touch you again.'

She laughed, a soft, rippling sound, and caressed the base of his neck beneath his collar with slow, sensual fingers. 'The helicopter will be waiting for us in exactly ninety minutes—and we'll be on our own. No one can interrupt us tonight. You're finally mine, Charlie Marandis— all of you. All mine.'

At the thought of the night, their eyes took fire, and they kissed with slow passion. Biding their time. Because it would come. And, from four feet away, Max smiled at the very private moment and turned away, as Jazmine had known he would.

Tonight was *not* royal time. Tonight they were just a man and woman in love, a groom and bride like any other. Tonight belonged to them alone, her wonderful firefighter lover and his little flower.

For the rest of her life, the world would have Kyriacou and Jazmine—but she'd have Charlie, and he'd have his *loulouthaki*.

For ever.

# MILLS & BOON PUBLISH EIGHT LARGE PRINT TITLES A MONTH. THESE ARE THE EIGHT TITLES FOR AUGUST 2009.

CR

## THE SPANISH BILLIONAIRE'S PREGNANT WIFE
Lynne Graham

## THE ITALIAN'S RUTHLESS MARRIAGE COMMAND
Helen Bianchin

## THE BRUNELLI BABY BARGAIN
Kim Lawrence

## THE FRENCH TYCOON'S PREGNANT MISTRESS
Abby Green

## DIAMOND IN THE ROUGH
Diana Palmer

## SECRET BABY, SURPRISE PARENTS
Liz Fielding

## THE REBEL KING
Melissa James

## NINE-TO-FIVE BRIDE
Jennie Adams

0809 Rom LP

# MILLS & BOON PUBLISH EIGHT LARGE PRINT TITLES A MONTH. THESE ARE THE EIGHT TITLES FOR SEPTEMBER 2009.

MILLS & BOON